The Frights

Nicholas Salaman was born in west Somerset, and educated at Radley and Oxford. He has written plays produced on television and the London stage, as well as a number of novels and children's books. He is married, lives in London, and plays the harpsichord.

NICHOLAS SALAMAN

THE FRIGHTS

HarperCollins*Publishers*

HarperCollins*Publishers*
77–85 Fulham Palace Road,
Hammersmith, London W6 8JB

This paperback edition 1994
1 3 5 7 9 8 6 4 2

Previously published in paperback by Grafton 1983
Reprinted fourteen times

First published in Great Britain by
The Alison Press/Martin Secker & Warburg Ltd 1981

Copyright © Nicholas Salaman 1981

The Author asserts the moral right to
be identified as the author of this work

ISBN 0 586 05607 6

Set in Times

Printed in Great Britain by
HarperCollinsManufacturing Glasgow

For my Mother who kept the frights at bay

'When the loop in time comes, and it does not come for everybody,
The hidden is revealed and the spectres show themselves.'

T.S. Eliot
The Family Reunion

'I am become death, the destroyer of worlds.'

R. Oppenheimer
quoting from the Hindu

PART ONE

1

The boys were playing in the labyrinth under the high laurel hedge that sloped down from the front drive to the abandoned tennis court.

'General Orange is mine.'

'No he isn't. Colonel Green's yours.'

'Colonel Green's only a Colonel. Why can't I have a General? Why can't Field Marshal Ball make him into a General?'

It was true, the younger brother always seemed to get the less impressive ranks in these games, or if not, the most moth-eaten of the Field Officers, but his brother always had a good reason. That was the advantage of being two and a half years older, and very nearly eight.

His brother had a good reason now.

'They're on different sides, stupid. My Field Marshal can't make your Colonel into a General. He's an enemy. You can't do that with enemies. Otherwise all the British Field Marshals would make all the Nazi ones into Privates, and no one in the German army would know who to take orders from. It would be unsporting.'

'Well, it's not fair. Why haven't I got a Field Marshal of my own? Why have I only got Colonel Green?'

'Because you're younger than I am.'

It was hot in the impenetrable shade under the laurels, and the younger boy was near to tears. His brother relented slightly for strategic considerations. He only liked emotional battles on his own terms.

'Very well. You have Field Marshal Ball, and I'll have Colonel Green, and we'll start all over again. You'll be sorry, though. Colonel Green's forces are much more manoeuvrable.'

9

So they should be. The truth was that Colonel Green's forces consisted solely of Colonel Green (a chipped skittle painted the colour of a Bramley Seedling with pompoms down its front) and a sort of knitted manikin of uncertain tactical advantage. Whereas the forces opposed to them were a brownish tennis ball, another chipped skittle (this time orange), a couple of roughly-daubed clothes-pegs, and a cloth baboon – a veteran assemblage of proven invincibility.

The younger brother, however, was not really interested in the game. He knew that whatever happened he would lose. He always did. The unfairness of it was that he never particularly wanted to win. He didn't like seeing the wrath and humiliation on his brother's intense little white face. But he hated losing.

'No. I don't want Field Marshall Ball.'

The tears started trickling down either side of his nose, reminding him of the Reverend Biddle, who came three times a week to give them lessons and who'd just launched into the subject of watersheds. The thought, however, gave him no particular comfort.

'Make up your mind,' said his brother, implacably. 'You don't want it one way and you don't want it the other. Which way do you want it?'

He didn't want it any way. He wanted the comfortable Nanny they'd left behind in Berkshire in the house they'd had to give up, beside the airfield.

'Oh come on,' said his brother. 'We've still got my counter-attack to come yet. If you don't stop blubbing and being such a hopeless ruin, I won't give you your Sleeping Draught tonight.'

2

Beyond the garden of the house, white with distempered pebbledash, pimply-glistening in the August sunshine, the woods stretched luscious, dank and mysterious.

On either side of the valley, the trees rose in ridge upon ridge, oak and rowan, silver birch and holly, some tall and well-turned-out, others bent and wrinkled, nevertheless between them giving the impression that they would be a decent and respectable forest were it not for that rabble of brambles and ferns and indeterminate saplings below stairs cluttering the floor and lowering the tone.

Beyond, on the other side of the hill towards Luxborough, there were thick woods of conifers standing so close you could hardly see ten yards, where you could lose yourself and no one would ever know, so the elder brother said. He also said that Rodgers the cowman had told him a corpse had been found up Sedgecombe way, must've been wandering a dozen days, Rodgers said, but Jackie Jewel said you don't want to go believing that old boy, bit too fond of the cider if you asked him, though it had also been said Jackie Jewel himself was not averse to a drop, so you didn't know who to believe.

The air in the valley, normally humid, was charged now with pollen and the beginnings of harvest dust, and hay-fever particles floated like incense. Wood-pigeon and grasshopper, cricket and cock-pheasant sang an endless canon from either side of the central meadows accompanied by occasional songs of graze from the Guernseys while an unnumbered congregation of midges formed and reformed in the shadows, intent on their endless offices under the trees.

The whole of Cutcombe lay in its own private ceremony of heat waiting for the evening to pronounce absolution.

It was half past noon, August 8th, 1942.

3

The grownups were gathered in the drawing-room of the pimply house for sherry before lunch under the eagle eye of the boys' grandmother, Old Mrs Sanderson, who sat in the middle of the big sofa, taking up all the room, while the rest of the party ranged themselves variously around her.

Apart from Chelly-Chops, her mainly-deaf companion who was really called Antoinette Chelford only everyone had forgotten, the company included the Granny's daughter-in-law, the beautiful Young Mrs Sanderson: Griselda, a squire's cast-off daughter from Northamptonshire: and Franco, her husband, an Italian artist who would have been interned if he hadn't been married to an English girl. Even so, he had only just scraped through – mainly due to the influence of the Granny, who liked to patronize the arts (and indeed everything else) and who, because she was a local JP, had had a word with the authorities, saying the couple could live under her eye, in the flat above her stables.

A couple of Americans from the local US Army Base down at St Paget's Bay had also turned up: Major Caldwell, a virile if somewhat apoplectic figure, and First Lieutenant Lippincott, of slighter build and more reflective feature.

The Reverend Biddle too had descended from Cutcombe Village, not in his fiery chariot (an aged Lea Francis which was only wheeled out these days to attend the urgently dying), but on his bicycle, attended by his sexton Georgie Taylor, secretary of the West Somerset Mummers.

They were discussing the party which was to be held the next Saturday down at the Base, an Open Evening of fraternization for the local medium-to-bigwigs and high jinks and frankfurters for the lesser wigs in the Village Hall.

'So,' the Granny was saying to Major Caldwell, who was second in command of the Base and clearly the one to talk to because Lieutenant Lippincott was only Education Officer and somewhat moony at that. 'So. Some kind of local participation would be most appropriate. A fitting seal . . . an affirmation of the Alliance . . . and what could be more appropriate than our Mummers performing at some stage in the evening? Old England greets the New World and so forth. A cabaret, forsooth, with a real Somerset flavour. A sword dance, the Langport Dragon, Jack o' the Green, Gathering Peascods . . . How say you, Major?'

The Granny had been an actress as a young girl until she had been swept away to a life of style in West Somerset by a dilettante Lochinvar who had once studied at the Slade and shared a girlfriend with Augustus John (although yielding her in the end to his superior brush work), but she still clung to her dramatic tricks of speech and her habit of wanting the best part on the best stage, which she had long ago decided was Cutcombe Hall.

Major Caldwell loosened his collar. It had been a glorious morning. The sun had danced on the little Cutcombe River as he had driven up, reminding him of the infinite shimmering reaches of his own Missouri, but as the morning had progressed it had become uncomfortably hot. He could feel his uniform licking his shoulderblades and, as he looked across at his hostess's daughter-in-law, he could feel it licking harder than ever.

Was it the done thing, he wondered, in the English

13

county set, to ask your hostess's daughter-in-law if she screwed before you had even so much as played a game of croquet?

The Granny was not to be put off.

'Hoots, mon,' she said in infuriating dialect, 'will ye no quit your havering?'

Major Caldwell smiled apologetically, restraining an impulse to say something unforgivable, a restraint which with him was both rare and unpleasant to look upon, his contused features not lending themselves kindly to the disciplines of tact.

'Well,' he said, 'I guess a little local colour at the party would be kind of cute.'

The Reverend Biddle winced.

'These ha dances,' he intoned, 'stem from the most immemorial antiquitah. They are traceable back to the ha terpsichorean fertilitah rituals of the primitive vegetation cults, still echoed today in the leaping ha phallic effigahs in Macedoniah, and so aptly described by Robert Graves in the White Goddess and so farth. Cute is hardly the ward I would have employed.'

'Gee,' said Major Caldwell, 'I'm sorry. I had no idea . . .'

But if there were going to be any leaping phalluses, he wouldn't mind leaping with the best of them, and he sure knew where he would leap when leaping-time was come.

'Mr Taylor heah and his colleagues, Prickard and Honeybone and Dawkins from Luxborough — though the youngah dancahs are now on active service and our faithful few remaining are not perhaps as limbah as they were — nevertheless, they still represent the unstoppable thrust of the earth farce. Is that not right, George?'

'Surely is, Reverend,' said Taylor, and began to hold forth on the significance of his staves.

Young Mrs Sanderson, mother of the two boys, though not the steatopygous figure of the Vegetation Cult

14

figurines, was nonetheless the subject of considerable worship, in the neighbourhood and sighed slightly, thinking not over-longingly of her clean-cut husband away in the army. The Son of Cutcombe goes forth to war, a kingly crown to gain. That's what the Granny had said anyway. It seemed rather hard to be on the loose for so long, but naturally one couldn't let Cutcombe down. Or could one? Those staves were fearfully compelling.

Griselda smiled encouragingly at Franco, hoping that he wasn't going to break into one of his ironic extravaganzas, and wishing that artists could behave a little more Burne-Jonesily.

Franco the Italian regarded an Augustus John which hung over the sideboard, a portrait of one of the Grand-father's sisters, and reflected on the fate of his own family back at home.

Chelly-Chops fiddled with her hearing aid. There seemed to be a great deal of static, which usually meant thunder around.

First Lieutenant Thomas Lippincott stood in a corner and regarded the mother with discreet veneration. A verse formed in his mind:

> Time seems congealed as scallop soup
> Located after some neglect
> Or running, like a film on loop.
> The Goddess comes. I genuflect.

As a former research graduate at the Massachusetts Institute of Technology studying quantum physics, it was hard to see what quirk of the Draft Board had appointed Thomas, at the age of twenty-six, to the post of Education and acting Intelligence Officer at the St Paget's Bay Gunnery and Weapons Training Base, but there it was: as with the nature of the universe, one couldn't always seek to know, one could only know to seek, and even that wasn't much good when it came to Draft Boards. He sometimes felt he might have been more usefully employed putting his nuclear training to good use back home, and sometimes (as he remembered just where his investigations had been leading) he felt extraordinarily glad that he wasn't.

He shivered at the recollection. A shadow seemed to fall across the bright polished parquet and deaden the intense viridian of the lawns. Hadn't he promised himself that he wouldn't think of all that for a while?

'Hoots toots and awa' wi' ye,' old Mrs Sanderson was crying roguishly as she instructed the Major in the essentials of the Sword Dance, somewhat to the annoyance of old Taylor, who was still in mid-symbol.

Lieutenant Lippincott glanced round quickly to make sure no one was taking any notice of him, and applied himself to his thoughts again, more cheering thoughts this time concerning his perennial loves, physics and poetry. Of course to a layman, the two subjects might have seemed a quirky combination, but to Lippincott there was no doubt that he had the very best of precedents. Had not the poet Donne been au fait with the latest scientific developments in his day, comparing lovers with pairs of compasses and invoking 'the skill of specular stone'? Had not Marvell made free play with planispheres and infinite parallel lines?

Though Dryden had accused them of 'perplexing the mind of the fair sex with metaphysical speculations', the poets of the seventeenth century had been enriched and inspired by the discoveries of the age's scientists.

Was it not incumbent on the poet today to be aware of the tremendous changes in thought that were taking place as Einstein, a second Newton, still living among them, mused on the implications of his discoveries in Space and Time?

In short, the idea of science providing imagery for the artist, and art kindling imagination in the scientist, appealed to Thomas, and it was, in fact, in the area of Space

16

and Time that they became most closely fused.

One of his professors back home had suggested that, as a corollary of the Theory of Relativity, Time could be considered as a particle-wave like Light. And pointing to the behaviour of a beam of light when shone at a board drilled with two holes – the light will permeate both perforations – he went on to moot that Time could be similarly 'dual' in its reactions when faced with an 'option'. Thus Time itself could be subject to fission, and be splitting with every microsecond that passed like candy-floss into a near-infinity of alternatives, so that the seed of every possibility in the Present could grow into a myriad different Futures. Hence, in one universe, it was the Allies who had won the Great War. In another, it was the Kaiser. In another, the war had never been fought at all. In another, the world had been destroyed by a wandering meteor long before.

These thoughts gave him the most delicious tremors of speculation. Even as he looked at the assembled company, he could not help imagining the multiplicity of outcomes that might emerge from so decent and well-regulated a gathering, where the very photographs of the grandparents and grandchildren provided seemingly irrefutable evidence of vertical single-stranded continuity.

Who knew? Things might not be what they seemed.

There was a knock on the door.

'Yes?' said Granny.

A buxom young woman in a striped gingham dress with a stiff white apron pitted against her ample bosom hovered by the door.

'Come in, Nanny-noo.'

But Nanny-noo kept hovering.

'I was looking for the boys,' she said. 'They just slipped away when my back was turned.'

She had been in her room trying out a new hairstyle.

'It's their lunchtime,' she said, looking at the Americans.

'Better try the shrubbery, Nanny,' said the Granny,

'that's where they usually get to. Playing soldiers like their father,' she explained to the Major and Lieutenant, who made appreciative mumbles as if to compliment her on her grandsons' pluck.

'Proper little eels they are sometimes. Thank you, Mrs Sanderson.'

She slid back round the door narrowly missing a mastectomy on the polished oak.

'Not quite the class of Nanny we used to have in the old days. A local girl with only the most vestigial training, but you simply can't get them now. One has to be grateful even for her. Willing enough, but frankly not Cutcombe calibre. But what can one do?'

The Reverend Biddle made a deprecating noise, but Major Caldwell knew exactly what one would like to do.

A gong sounded somewhere back in the house.

'You will stay to lunch?' said the Granny. 'Pot luck, I'm afraid, with the rationing what it is, but we usually manage to scratch up an edible morsel.'

4

Tristram Sanderson, in a room of oppressive heat (with the thunder bouncing and growling outside) under a bright bath of electric light from the obligatory single bulb, was being interrogated by the Gestapo, but he didn't mind too much because anything in the world was better than jumping out of aeroplanes.

Parachuting was the worst thing ever invented, and he knew that if he had to do it once more, his stomach would do a double sheepshank with disastrous internal consequences before he even got out of the Lancaster's trapdoor. But he couldn't tell anyone, of course, because when you were the Son of Cutcombe you couldn't go whingeing around complaining and being weedy. You could never look your clean-cut features in the shaving mirror again. Mind you, it didn't look from here as if either jumping or shaving mirrors were going to be very much on the cards in future.

'I say, old boy.' His inquisitor slapped him hard on the face with his exquisitely tailored glove. 'Pay attention when I talk to you. With whom were you attempting to make contact? Who is the head of the Resistance in Rouen? What did you do with your papers?'

'I am only obliged to give you my name, rank, number and unit. These details I believe you have at the present time.'

'Present, present. There is no such thing as present. The present is only a machine for turning the future into the past. A machine, I may say, from which we are not extracting maximum efficiency at the moment, my friend. Do not quote Geneva Conventions at me, old boy.' Another stinging slap was delivered. 'You come like a thief in the night, wearing no uniform, bearing no invitation, yes, that is it, you come like a gate-crasher, so you must not be surprised if the bouncers are over-zealous with you.'

Tristram wanted to say that in England only girls slapped chaps' faces but thought it might only invite more robust disapprobation.

'Come now,' continued the officer, 'why not make it easy for yourself? Tell us what we want to know and no one will ever discover that it was you who spilled the beans. Otherwise we might have to become somewhat more Draconian in our approach.'

Tristram was glad he hadn't talked about English girls, but he still seemed to be rather in the soup. Where on earth had this Gestapo fellow been educated? Clearly he had

19

spent some time in England, perhaps a public school, possibly even Winchester — he spoke with that fastidious precision that sounds as though the tongue's got rubber gloves on.

The Gestapo officer seemed to be reading his thoughts.

'Oxford, old boy. Brasenose for two years reading PPE. Must talk about it some time. Trouble is, we have more pressing matters on our hands at the moment. Chief among which seems to be that you do not appear to be telling the truth. Oh, I know what you are going to say . . .'

Tristram wasn't going to say anything. Quite the reverse. He was very willing for the German to rattle on all day. He could tell him about his early childhood in the Black Forest if he liked.

'You are going to tell me that truth is a very relative matter . . .'

Tristram had to admit to himself that this would have been in less oppressive circumstances quite a witty line to take, but as it was, he flapped a vaguely deprecating hand.

'Oh yes, I have heard it postulated in more tutorials than you're going to have hot dinners, old boy, that Truth is a highly subjective commodity. What is Truth, said Pilate, jesting, and would not stay for an answer, what? And then there's your Bishop Berkeley with his axiom that nothing exists except in the senses of the observer. Hence there can be any number of possible truths because there can be any number of possible spectators . . . Oh, I enjoy a philosophical chinwag. Captain Sanderson, as you see, reminding me of those jolly far-off undergrad days. Now, if we were to accept the Berkeleian argument you have advanced . . .'

He paused, cocking his head a little to one side as if to encourage Tristram to chip in, an invitation Tristram decided to decline. Clearly his inquisitor enjoyed the sound of his own voice.

The thunder seemed to be getting closer, but it might just

as well have been the Anna Magdalena Notenbuch played by a neighbour's fifteen-year-old daughter for all the notice the officer took of it.

'If we were to accept that thesis,' the German continued, quite unmoved by Tristram's lack of response, 'we might also accept that there is some truth in the story you have told me, for your truth would have just as much validity as mine. But . . . ' suddenly another slap was administered which made Tristram's eyes water ' . . . but, Captain Sanderson, we are living in somewhat more empirical times. These are not the groves of academe. And even if they were I would remind you of the refutation of Bishop Berkeley's argument: "There was a young man who said God, must find it exceedingly odd, to see that a tree, continues to be, when there's no one around in the Quad." '

The man, as well as being almost certifiably obsessed with himself, was plainly a Grade One cad. But Tristram couldn't help shivering. He was not in a situation where judgements of this sort held much water. It would have been different had it been a Meet of the West Somerset Foxhounds.

'So, Captain Sanderson, let us concur that we appear at the moment to be inhabiting the same continuum in which we can agree that a tree is a tree, and that Truth is Truth, and that you at this moment do not appear to be telling it. In which case, Captain Sanderson, I can only reach one conclusion. It is that you are lying. Lying, lying, lying. And if you value your hide, I strongly advise you for the last time: if you have the beans, spill them. There is going to be an invasion is there not? Now . . . where is it to be? Normandy: Brittany? Les haricots, Captain Sanderson . . . Versez donc.'

Tristram, who was more tired than he could remember ever having been in his life, forced his mind back to dwell on his predicament. If he didn't look sharp it wouldn't be the beans he would be spilling but the contents of his small or indeed large intestines torn apart by a burst of fifty rounds rapid fire from a shrewdly-aimed Schmeisser, or his cranium, after a truncheon session, smashed into little bits the way he had seen them cook goats in Jamaica.

First things first. Play for time, he thought, that was the ticket. There was a procedure they'd taught him back at Training for this sort of thing.

'Before we continue with your conversation,' he said, noting that the officer was already shuffling his papers again, 'perhaps I might be permitted a small . . . half-time. I feel it might help to bring back one or two things that previously seemed to have slipped my mind. I mean, all this war seems to be about is a few Jews and Poles. The Germans and the English really ought to be fighting the Russians.'

'Excellent, Captain. Capital. You're a sensible fellow.'

'Thing is, feeling a bit muzzy. Wonder if it'd be possible to continue our chat after I've had a rest. And I'd give anything for a cup of tea.'

The officer looked at him intently, gave an order to the soldier, and stood up.

'Tea, forsooth, the English riposte to all the thrusts of Fortune. Very well, Captain,' he said. 'We will resume our talk when you have rested a little and had some refreshment. I fear I cannot guarantee cucumber sandwiches but we will do our best. You may lie on the bed if you wish. I can only allow you an hour or two but, meanwhile, pleasant dreams.'

With that he turned off the light and left the room, and Tristram, lying down on the truckle bed in the corner, shut his eyes and tried to concentrate on his predicament.

5

Down in the summerhouse which looked like a gingerbread
cottage among the rhododendrons on the lower lawn where
nobody went, the boys' mother was entertaining Major
Caldwell.

The key to the little two-storey witching-house had, as
far as most people knew, been lost for years. Nobody ever
needed to get in there these days since all it contained was
rotten deckchairs, a disintegrating tennis-net and a clutch
of spoon-shaped rackets. The Mother had discovered it
some time ago as the one place near the house you could be
sure of not being overrun by the Granny, so she had
appropriated the key and hidden it beneath the velvet
cushion of the second unfold of her jewellery box under the
boring garnets which not even Chelly-Chops would rifle,
only removing it when she had an urge for absolute privacy,
an urge that she felt sweeping across her with increasing
velocity these days.

Down here, though, there was no fear of her being
disturbed, since only Ferdy Fowler had ever had the other
key, and that was lost behind a string of impenetrable
corms in his potting shed.

When Major Caldwell had suggested a stroll after lunch,
she had agreed with an alacrity that surprised both of them.
Everyone else seemed sunk in post-prandial lethargy
(Granny's morsel had turned out to include garden peas,
new potatoes and Cutcombe capon), although Lieutenant
Lippincott's face had suffered something of a landslide
when they announced they were going to inspect the
garden, in a tone of voice that precluded any suggestion of
additional company. The rest of their progress had had a

23

sort of dreamlike inevitability to it.

Major Caldwell ('call me Chuck') had taken her to his jeep, extracted a bottle of bourbon and a pair of silk stockings which lived permanently under the seat in anticipation of such an emergency, and blandished her with a promise that they might take a trip down to Blue Anchor tomorrow for a swim because thanks to his role as Officer in Charge of the Officer in Charge of Camp Transport he could put the gas they used down to evaporation in the storage tanks.

The mother did not like to be churlish in these matters. She accepted the gifts and the invitation, and slipped up to collect the key and visit the larder for ice while Queenie the kitchenmaid was having her afternoon nap.

And then she had led him down through the rhododendrons, under the wistaria, past the cobwebs and into the gingerbread sanctum whose windows only admitted privileged slivers of dusty afternoon sunlight.

Safely inside, she locked the door, set out the glasses and the ice, and splashed on the Wild Turkey with reckless precision.

'Isn't this fun?' she said. 'Like a midnight feast.'

And a little later, fired as much by the months of boredom as by the mouthfuls of bourbon, she invited him upstairs to the witch's bedroom where there was an old Rajah Brookish cane sofa, to see how the stockings fitted.

They fitted very well indeed.

'Honey,' said Major Chuck who was a leg man though he liked boobs as well, 'back where I come from, if a girl had legs like that, she'd never need to use them for walking. She'd have a string of Cadillacs and Studebakers parked from Minneapolis to St Paul waiting for the chance to take her from the swimming pool to the cocktail closet. Where I come from . . .'

But the mother (whose name was Julia) was bored with Major Chuck's Mid-Western reminiscences and wanted to get on with the next bit. The Major might not be exactly Ivy League but he was a fine figure of a Major.

That was better. He was beginning to knead her foot.

'Let me be your transport officer,' he said avidly, 'and I'll give you a rundown of one or two little detours I thought we might investigate.'

'Tell me about it later,' suggested the Mother, allowing the Major to run his paws up the lissom undulations of her knees, and noticing with a sort of excited distaste the stain spreading across the khaki under each of Major Chuck's ham-like armpits.

He was crouching in front of her now, and she adjusted her knees to accommodate his addresses. His hands glissaded up her thighs and tumbled about among the nursery-slopes above her stocking welts. In spite of herself and her emotional indifference to Major Chuck, she gasped. She could never get used to the suddenness of pleasure. She was glad he was so involved down there with her pins and couldn't see her face.

She never knew how to look at these moments.

'Honey,' cried Major Chuck again, burying his face in the rather expensive French knickers that someone else had given her, and indeed she smelt as sweet as a bee.

Julia was very beautiful. Her dark hair, her boyish features, her capricious self-centredness, her vulnerable mouth, her slender legs, her slightly too heavy bosom, her enjoyment of love-making, would all individually have commanded a substantial following, and combined had enslaved half the county. She looked like a delinquent Alice Liddell.

Many girls have a deceptive fecklessness and misty irresponsibility in youth, and before the crags of character show, should have a notice round their necks, 'Running in – please pass', to warn prospective husbands.

But Julia had gone on running in. Character she certainly had but she couldn't react to maturity seriously. Now at thirty-two, with two boys age seven and five, and a husband away playing secret war games with the Intelligence Corps, she could only feel that she was in a state of terrible waste. Here she was at the very apogee of her beauty, and there was no one to enjoy it, and who knew how long the war might go on. She was still the most beautiful woman within a radius of twenty miles, and she saw no reason why time should be allowed to ruin something that others could well be appreciating.

'When time starts to spoil the spoilt,' someone had once said to her, 'everyone else stops doing so.'

It hadn't been said as a compliment, but it was undeniably true. The war had put paid to so much fun, she was damned if it was going to rob her of all that lovely power − because it was the power she liked best, the absolute despotism she could wield over her admirers, the fealty she could command from her serviceable villeins.

Not that sex was meaningless to her, but she was one of those rare and fortunate women who could (as men are commonly supposed to) enjoy sex without emotional attachment.

'Ah.'

That was nice. Her thighs had always been sensitive. Clearly the Major had learned something from his ten years of Mississippi marriage or wherever it was. She could feel herself blossoming like one of those films, shot at slow-motion, of flowers opening to the tropic sun.

'Heliotrope,' she said.

'What's that?' said the Major muffledly.

'Don't stop.'

The boys, of course, were a problem.

She would be the first to admit that she was no good with children. She didn't understand them, little boys specially. They bored her. She had only had them because it was the done thing, expected of the Son of Cutcombe, and that was before the war started. So now, with no husband on hand, virtually no staff and only that half-trained miller's daughter to look after them, they had become more and more her responsibility — a responsibility which characteristically she did everything in her power to avoid.

'Running in — please pass.' Somebody had said that to her once. A lot of people had said a lot of things to her in anger, chagrin or disappointment because her angelic appearance did rather suggest that a Uriel might lurk within. No such luck, of course, Uriels being in short supply like everything else these days.

The Major did not seem to mind, however, as he removed her knickers with something between a sob and a whoop.

Julia found it heightened her purely physical sensations to let her mind wander while making love. It did not make her a particularly participative partner but she was far too succulent for it to worry her lovers by even so much as a whisker. So once again she allowed her attention to drift over her predicament. Something would have to be done about those boys, of course.

In September, Rufus would go to boarding school, and Adam . . . well, something could be found for Adam. If only Tristram would pull his weight when he came home on leave instead of wandering about like an absent-minded Narcissus. It was too bad of Tristram. Certainly his soldiering might be taxing, all that cloak and dagger stuff, but it was better than being blown up in your Churchill in the Western Desert like her cousin Robert. What did he want to be so cagey about?

Her nipples felt like fuchsias as the Major tried to pop them in his mouth.

But she had given up with Tristram. She knew, she alone knew, that the Son of Cutcombe wasn't all he was cracked up to be.

Her thoughts moved on to a little more self-commiseration. It wasn't easy for her, suddenly having to move out of

27

their nice house near Abingdon, and come down to this mausoleum in the wilds of Somerset.

She had got on well with the Old Sanderson when he was alive. He said she reminded him of the girl he'd vied for with Augustus John.

'Sometimes,' he used to say, 'I think you're my Dorelia come back to me.'

But the old boy was dead now and the dread dragon ruled the roost. Thank God she more or less confined herself to the house, though you never quite knew where she was going to crop up. Mind you, she found it remarkably easy to ignore her. The Granny was so used to addressing the gallery, one could sort of slide along out of sight under the footlights.

The Major was running in now and she could hear his heart thudding like an old hunter as he approached the jump.

Why had she married Tristram? The question often bothered her. It was really her father's fault, she felt. He was an impecunious author, absent-minded, unsuccessful, indigent, and not infrequently drunk; her mother simply couldn't cope and devoted her time to the garden. Her home, therefore, had been dowdy, raffish and considerably doom-laden. The vegetables had been fine but that didn't seem really to compensate.

Meeting the Son of Cutcombe, and coming down for a weekend to the Lodge had been a revelation. The Son so dashing, and clean-cut, and popular, and the Father so civilized and with such an eye for the finer things which included her belle poitrine. It was wonderful, it was magical, it was everything her home had never been.

'This way, do it this way,' she adjured the beavering Major, who appeared to be slightly off course.

And so they had got married. Not that she had not had other offers, but the features of the man, and the magic of the place, and the easy familiarity with Lord and Lady St

Paget, and the Mohuns over at Combe Barton, and the Luttrells at Dunster had worked their spells upon, if not her heart, at least her judgement.

It was only afterwards, and not very long afterwards at that, that she had discovered her dashing white sergeant was, under all that county effortlessness and genial arrogance, a secret artist himself. He kept a diary. That was suspicious. He drew flowers or things in a book. That was unforgivable.

She kept it quiet naturally, and he didn't tell anyone about it, so she let it ride. But she knew, she knew. He was a masquerader. She couldn't trust him any more.

The Major appeared to be reaching projection now, and was making noises like a precipitating crucible.

If she had caught Tristram in bed with another woman, she couldn't have felt more let down. An artist − after all she had promised herself − after she had seen what her mother suffered. An artist! Not, of course, that he was a full-time practitioner, that would have been grounds for separation, but knowing that he might be sneaking off and being unfaithful to her like this when she thought he might've just gone for a walk, that was bad enough. And it worked on her affections like the slow onset of winter. He was also exceedingly bad in bed.

She abandoned her unsatisfactory thoughts and devoted herself to the mazy rhythms of the moment, writhing and bopping to the Major's spritely measure.

If she didn't watch out she was going to be late for tea, but it didn't seem to matter as the Officer in Charge of the Transport Officer pumped thousands of gallons into her tender.

6

Mealtimes at Cutcombe Hall came round thick and fast, even though there was a war on. One had, of course, to make sacrifices, but it didn't mean to say one had to eat burnt offerings.

Granny Sanderson enjoyed her food, and now, thank goodness, it was teatime again.

She always particularly relished tea. The dining-room so lent itself to the occasion. The mahogany sideboard, the great oak table, the Spode service, the portraits on the walls, even the Italian's recent picture of the two little boys seemed to lend a sense of tradition and unruffledness to the ceremony.

She might not be as nimble as she used to be, but she could still enjoy the ritual of the massive silver apparatus with the methylated burner to keep the water hot, beside which she sat, upstaging the rest of the table. And she could still put away the Cutcombe cream and the Cutcombe butter and the Cutcombe honey on the Cutcombe home-made scones like nobody's business.

It was strange indeed that such a succulent enjoyment of the pleasures of the table should attend such a sharpness of tongue and so critical an eye, but there it was. No doubt Lucretia Borgia enjoyed her food.

'Most toothsome,' she praised the clotted cream bowl. 'The crust is astonishingly brittle. But then of course Cutcombe cream was always noted for being the best in the whole of Williton Hundred. I remember when your Grand-father and I first came here . . .'

The boys were allowed to have tea with the grownups, taking their other meals in the cream-and-green nursery under the gaze of the miller's daughter.

Granny always knew that everything Cutcombe was best. Cutcombe cream. Cutcombe greengages and goosegogs, Cutcombe vegetables, Cutcombe peaches and grapes tended with loving observance by old Ferdy Fowler in the greenhouse, and (Adam suddenly remembered with a tweak of guilt) Cutcombe figs.

'A fig for your thoughts, Adam,' Granny was watching him beadily over the silver scaffolding of the tea-machinery, its little blue flame winking like a familiar.

Why was it Granny always knew what you were thinking, always unfailingly found you out? There had been that business of the pane of glass in the scullery he had bashed with Field Marshal Ball. It could have been anybody. It could just have happened. It was only a small crack — why shouldn't glass just break? But Granny knew unerringly that it was Adam. And now it was the figs.

It was jolly unfair really. It had been Rufus's idea, and as usual Rufus had got him to do the dirty work.

They were beautiful figs, bulging green and big as toads, with a sweet juicy pippiness that made you water at the mouth just to think of them. There were so many of them too. Typical of Granny to know that one had gone. She must have had Ferdy Fowler counting the ripe ones for her every single day. She wanted them for her breakfast. Cutcombe figs, singularly toothsome . . .

He looked at his plate and hoped something would happen. Perhaps the meths container would explode. Perhaps there'd be a dogfight like there'd been once, a Spitfire and a Messerschmitt high overhead, and they'd all go out and look in the garden.

But Granny was peering at him with those terrible watery bright agaty eyes.

'It was you, wasn't it, Adam?' she said, her displeasure turning the cream and honey to acid and vinegar in her mouth. 'It was you who picked the fig. You know what happens to little boys who steal. They get sent away, with a label round their necks, don't they? I won't have little thieves in my house.'

Adam panicked. He always disliked this train of argument. He had a fear of being mislaid somewhere in the North.

'It wasn't my . . .' he began, but stopped, seeing his brother sitting very still and regarding him intently, head to one side like a robin.

'It's unfair,' he tried again. 'It was . . . ' but he stopped once more. How did one explain?

'Don't try and wriggle out of it,' said Granny, liberally helping herself to crab-apple jelly, 'if there's one thing worse than a thief, it's a liar. Get down from the table and go to the Nursery at once. I'm not going to have little criminals at my teatable. Cut along now.'

Thank goodness those Americans weren't here to see his shame, he thought, not daring to finish his last bite of cucumber sandwich (Cutcombe cukes, best in the Universe).

Adam slipped from his chair and padded miserably across the dining-room, past the heavily carved black sideboard with the gargoyles on each end, grinning in the face of his humiliation, observers of the latter end of goodness knew how many kippered herrings and devilled kidneys, and out through the heavy polished cedar door, brought back by Grandfather from the Lebanon, tears bubbling up from his seemingly inexhaustible reservoirs of grief.

What was it Nanny had said to her sister up from Bristol? 'Won't need to worry about the seas running dry. Not with that one around.' He'd listened behind the door when they thought he was in the bath. How could they know what it felt like to be small, in someone else's house, being treated like a sort of feeble-minded criminal pygmy? And anyway, there was no danger the seas would run dry, was there? So only a feeble-minded grownup would worry about that.

There was silence in the dining-room until the door had almost closed behind him, and then he heard the Grandmother addressing Chelly-Chops, who had been juggling all through tea with her hearing-aid batteries which hung in copious nursing brassieres on either side of her thin chests, Chelly-Chops who had sat as she always did when trouble was in the air, on the edge of her seat, malignantly eager not to miss a word.

'SPEAK ROUGHLY TO YOUR LITTLE BOY, AND BEAT HIM WHEN HE SNEEZES . . . ' said Granny.

'Little turk. Nasty brutes, boys,' replied Chelly-Chops, catching the drift but flicking the switches of her instrument in hope of catching a bit more.

Adam met his mother coming through the front door as he turned to mount the stairs. She was smoothing her skirt and running a vague hand through the ripples of her hair.

'Oh really, Adam. You always seem to be blubbing these days. What on earth's the matter?'

'I . . . I . . . '

'You must try not to be so sensitive.'

Sensitive was the most terrible crime, it seemed, as far as grownups were concerned — sensitive was something prawn-eyed Masters of Foxhounds had shaken off in the bassinet.

But his mother didn't stop to discuss the situation. As Adam trudged up the final flight of stairs to the very top of the house, and Major Chuck slipped glibly through the shrubbery towards his waiting jeep, she was already aggravating Granny by ignoring her sarcastic remarks about maybe being somewhat late for tea but perhaps a morsel early for dinner and what was the use of telling the servants that meals would be served at certain hours if certain people couldn't be bothered to turn up, and piling her scone high with cream and whortleberry jelly because lovemaking always made her peckish.

33

'Sorry, Granny,' she said, 'completely lost track of time. Can't think what came over me.'

Chelly-Chops, who missed very little of what went on in Cutcombe circles, choked imperceptibly over her rock-cake.

7

Nanny, of course, was not properly a Nanny at all, not in the old wash-your-mouth-out-with-soap school, though she tried to learn the immemorial lines from Nanny Fairfax whenever they visited the Fairfaxes over at Combe Huish (visits that because of the petrol shortage were becoming ever fewer and further between); no, really Nanny was the daughter of Old Anstey, the local miller who had sent her, just before the war, to train as a secretary in Bristol.

Before she had fully mastered her Imperial or had discovered even the rudiments of shorthand, she had been sent home on the occasion of the first serious air-raid, and been kicking her heels thereafter down in the village, until Granny with her usual mixture of nest-feathering and busybodydom had scooped her up to minister to the Cutcombe grandchildren.

Nanny had a gentleman friend who was in the desert at the moment, but it didn't stop her having another one who wasn't. It didn't, as a matter of fact, stop her from having every able-bodied man in the district and one or two lame ones beside (which was one of the reasons Old Anstey had been glad to find her a job where she could get into as little mischief as possible). But the truth was that she was much more cut out for gentlemen friends than she was for looking after little boys, because she had a pretty face and large

Brie-like breasts which weren't much use to the under-tens.

She wasn't exactly an unpleasant creature, vain perhaps, idle certainly, but it all added up to yet another blot on the Cutcombe landscape like Marmaduke the gander, to be skirted cautiously.

Adam opened the door of the Nursery, and discovered Nanny gazing out of the window with an expression of vacuous unfulfilment. She was just thinking of Rodgers the cowman and those capable hands of his tugging at the teats in the musky half-light of the byre, and wishing that he would tug now, this instant, at hers, when the rattle of the handle disturbed her reverie.

On seeing Adam, she was understandably vexed.

'Adam?' What you doing here, then? You'm meant to be at tea. Your Gran'll skin you alive.'

Adam told her what had happened in the dining-room.

'Always in trouble, that's what you are. Regular little mischief. Turn my back for five minutes and there you are up to your neck. Ought to be ashamed, you ought. You don't seem to realize what your Gran's, I mean Granny's, doing for you. Think of the refugees and be thankful you're not one of them with a label round your neck and no one to call your own.'

But it was she, she knew, who ought to feel ashamed, having those shocking thoughts about Rodgers, rolling in the straw, frock up round her thighs, thrashing about in the midden, while he plied her with those terrible hands.

Why wouldn't the boy leave her alone? Still, it was a little hard on the child.

'You best go to your room and draw the curtains. Can't sit here, then, can you? Don't want your Gran to think I'm too easy on you,' she concluded in a gentler but still lust-thickened voice.

8

The bedroom was just along the passage past the little window and the prints from Sylvie and Bruno, and next door to the bathroom with the single big tap that drip-drip-dripped leaving a big red Somerset stain on the enamel.

The room was painted blue, with white on the ceiling and skirting-boards, and its blueness was echoed by a clammy linoleum floor on which stood a white chest and three white chairs (one for each of the boys and one for a visitor) and two low wooden beds with patchwork counterpanes, one near the door and the other in the far corner, which was Adam's.

Rufus had a room of his own next door now, a more grownup sort of room, but because it faced west he would still come in every morning, and they would look out of the single sash window, across the back lawn and beyond the kitchen garden, to where the hills rose in big bap-like folds to the east, to see what sort of day it was going to be. (It had been a bad day today but you couldn't blame that on Red Sky in the Morning.)

Adam inspected the picture of Captain Hook and the pirates. There appeared to be twelve of them today, yesterday it had been fourteen, but he didn't feel in the mood for a recount. For all he cared there could be 999 pirates next time he looked. For all he cared the house could burn down with Captain Hook and the pirates and Sylvie and Bruno and Nanny and Granny and Chelly-Chops and the whole bang lot of them. Even in his mood of hard-done-by depression, however, he felt this might be too desperate an outcome, so he stopped thinking about it in case it might happen. He rather liked Sylvie and Bruno.

So he took off his shoes and socks, lay on his bed and played with the long hanging pompom of the light switch, blipping it so it swung this way and that, seeing how long it would swing before he had to blip it again. If he did it for long enough he could go into a sort of trance. He felt better now. Nobody would come and get at him in his bedroom, not by day anyway.

The nights were a different matter.

As he slipped under the to-and-fro spell of the light cord, he thought drowsily of the first time he had heard about the Frights.

It was seven o'clock a couple of months ago, looking out at the Shepherd's Warning over a discussion concerning the day's curriculum that his brother had first raised the subject.

'Red sky in the morning,' Rufus had said, adding unnecessarily because Adam had known what it meant: 'That means it's going to rain. I vote we play soldiers in the attic.'

'I don't think I want to.'

Adam didn't exactly enjoy being awkward, but neither did he feel he should necessarily fall in with everything his brother suggested. He didn't see why, just because he was nearly three years younger, he should always have to be jostled into things. Why did Rufus always have such definite ideas on what he wanted to do anyway? Life for Adam was a much vaguer affair, to be spent on the spur of the moment, pottering about by oneself, waggling the mouths of the snapdragons, popping the fuchsia pods or playing catapults with the plantains. He didn't like the more formal regimented games his brother enjoyed: for one thing he always lost, for another Rufus always so much loved winning and greeted it rather in the manner with which the Granny approached clotted cream, with a loud and succulent relish.

'You jolly well do as I say.'

'Why should I?'

37

The pattern of these arguments was predictable, the sudden heat, the lapse into stalemate.

'Because I'm older than you.'

Adam had suddenly spotted a rare dialectical opportunity.

'That's no reason. Nanny's older than you and you don't always do what she says.'

The sudden unexpected shaft upset Rufus. His white face flushed and his eyes narrowed dangerously.

'That's different.'

But Adam had been emboldened by his sudden polemical success, and now discovered an unusual vein of stubbornness.

'Well I won't anyway and that's that.'

Rufus's eyes glowed like tracer bullets.

'I'm warning you.'

Adam was suddenly frightened. There was a side of Rufus that was unpredictable, that could sometimes be violent in a pinched-white sort of way. He now stared at Adam in ominous silence.

'NANNY,' Adam faltered.

But Nanny was still locked in the arms of Morpheus (which was what, with a twinkle at her own erudition, Granny called being asleep).

Adam looked at his brother in helpless fascination. The next step was usually a beating-up from a Rufus so inspired by fury that he would simply lay into him speechlessly for a minute or two or hurl him like a sack of potatoes onto one or other of the beds.

On this occasion, however, Rufus found words — though when they came, Adam felt he would have preferred any amount of pummelling.

'Nanny won't help you. She's probably in league with them.'

Adam felt a plummet of dismay in his stomach even though he had no idea what his brother was talking about.

There was something horribly ominous about the 'Them'.

'In league? In league with who?'

'Ah. That would be telling.'

Rufus looked like a demented pixie as he once again took the conversational initiative. He had not forgiven Adam for his brief reversal, and, to teach him a lesson, set about terrifying him with the very spectres that haunted the back of his own imaginings, the very worst ones, right at the back, and serve him right.

'Go on. Tell me.'

'You'd be too frightened.'

'No I wouldn't.'

Adam knew he would be, but he wanted to hear all the same. That was the terrible thing about Rufus's mysteries, they caught at you like riverweed.

'All right, then. The Frights.'

'The Frights?'

The name woke in Adam a particular and inescapable dread, as though all his life he had been waiting for it. The Frights? Where had he heard it before? And didn't he know in some inexplicable but totally insistent way what they looked like, what sound they made?

'I think she knows them. I've been watching her.'

Rufus knew he had scored a hit, but his satisfaction didn't persuade him to be lenient. He watched Adam's concern with clinical hatred, like old Holmes-Smith the dentist doing a filling. Adam for his part knew he ought not to react, which was the only way of dealing with his brother's goadings, but as usual the impulse was too much for him.

'Who . . . who are the Frights?'

'Better not to talk about them,' Rufus lowered his voice. 'They only come at night . . . but you never know. You can't describe them. Freaks. Some have wings. They all have claws. They have . . . faces. Their leader . . . ' his foice was barely audible ' . . . a sort of owl. They come in

39

the night. And if children are awake, they take them away . . .'

Adam blenched. He was horribly afraid of the dark; in fact he'd only just grown out of needing a night-light. Now he knew what he was afraid of – the rustlings, the creakings, the flappings at the window – he'd sensed all along that the night was full of things that were out to snatch him, in spite of what the grownups might say. And here was his brother, who had much more reason to know about it, being small and therefore more in the front line against monsters, lunatics and nightwalkers, confirming his worst fears.

'But what if you wake up?'

'What if *I* wake up?'

'I mean . . . what if *I* wake up?'

'That's just the point. You jolly well would – and they'd take you.'

'Take me . . . where?'

'Nobody knows. Wherever it is they come from. The one thing that's certain is you'd never be seen again.'

Adam, with bounding heart, approached the most crucial question of all.

'Why don't they take me, Rufus?'

'They would, of course they would – because you'd be bound to wake up sooner or later. But luckily for you, I give you a Sleeping Draught.'

Adam examined this revelation for a minute or two, probing it for flaws.

'I never see you give me a Sleeping Draught.'

'That doesn't mean I don't give it to you.'

'How?'

'I put it in your Ovaltine or cereal at supper, changing to avoid suspicion. If the grownups knew they'd stop me, and then you'd be for the high-jump.'

Adam considered the matter a little more. Thank goodness he liked Ovaltine and always finished it – cereal too, it didn't have gristly lumps in it. But he still felt there were one or two things that needed explaining. His emotions told him Rufus was right but he detected one or two rational flaws.

'Why don't lots of children get taken?'

'They do.'

'Well, why don't people hear about it?'

'It's all hushed up or there'd be panic.'

'I . . . I don't believe you. You're making it up.'

'Very well. I won't give it to you tonight. Then you'll see.'

'I'll . . . I'll tell Mother.'

'The person who gave me the Sleeping Draught, a friend, says that no one must be told, or the Frights will get wind of it and find a way of stopping him, and then you really would be for it. We both would. I take it myself, of course. I administer it to myself.'

Rufus was so intent, so moved by what he was saying, that Adam found his astonishing disclosure totally plausible. No little boy of seven and three quarters could possibly invent a story like that.

He allowed his thoughts another peep over the edge of his brother's revelation. He wanted to know more, and yet he was desperately sorry he'd been told anything at all. A thought had occurred to him, however, which needed settling.

'What do the Frights do with the children?'

'No one knows. They never come back. A boy was once found wandering in the woods, but they'd taken away his moral fibre, and he died soon afterwards. It's believed they use them as slaves and work them in the dark till they drop. Or take them to the torture chambers and do things with tweezers. But I think it's better not to know.'

The Granny was always stressing the importance of moral fibre, so that cutting-off of it was clearly the grossest kind of act, and Adam reacted with a due measure of awe.

41

It was like being an evacuee without a label. He felt he'd never sleep again.

'That's why I think it'd be a rather good thing, actually,' his brother continued, 'if you did decide to come and play soldiers in the attic today. I'd be much more likely to agree to go on giving you the Sleeping Draught. Otherwise I can't help feeling it might slip my mind.'

Adam was impressed by this argument, so impressed that for two months now he had been obedient to Rufus's almost every whim. To avoid being spirited from his snug bed in the middle of the night to heaven knew what nasty destination, it seemed silly not to acquiesce to French cricket on the old tennis court, everlasting campaigns with Colonel Green and Co. in the shrubbery, the Battle of Trafalgar on the little stream that ran down through the woods from Cutcombe Quarry, Field Cooking of potatoes on the clay oven that their father had built when he was a boy up in the paddock beyond the kitchen garden, or even taking the blame for Rufus when Field Marshal Ball serving in his dual capacity as projectile most incontinently leapt up and broke the scullery window.

On the whole, knowing there was no alternative, that he had to go along with everything Rufus dictated, Adam had accepted the situation phlegmatically. It was a relief in some ways having things decided for you, and not having to assert your personality all the time. Personality was on his mind because the Reverend Biddle had given a sermon on the subject last Sunday indicating that the loss of Personality (as opposed to Moral Fibre) might not be such a bad thing.

'Personaliteh,' the Reverend had declared in rolling tones, 'personaliteh is the outward dress, the noiseh fashion, the monkey chattah, the greedeh postuah, the empteh dogma of self-love. The Italians have personaliteh. They are volatile. They are colourful. They are perhaps a little flasheh. But when the cards are on the table as they are today, where does their personaliteh land them? They are drubbed out of Greece. They are harried in Ethiopiah. They are hounded the length and breadth of their own Mediterranean Sea. You ask me why? I will tell you.' He would even if you didn't. 'They have cultivated Personaliteh at the expense of Charactah. Charactah is the strength inside. Charactah enduahs. Charactah rides the storm. Charactah bites the bullet. Charactah is the very fabric of the British Empire. It climbed the heights of Abraham. It survived the Black Hole of Calcuttah. It went with Scott to the Antarctic, and it hurled the solitareh Spitfiah at the hellish hordes of the Hun . . .'

So Adam reasoned that by subduing himself, he wasn't just pleasing Rufus, he was getting into God's good books as well.

Just once or twice there had been moments of rebellion, but a meaning look from his brother and the dire caution 'NSD' (No Sleeping Draught) soon had him coming round again.

It didn't stop him worrying about the Frights, though. The mornings weren't so bad; you could almost believe they never existed. The early afternoons were bold and bright, and you were too happy at having got through another lunch of gristly Irish stew, fibrous vegetable marrows and tapioca to worry about the slowly lengthening shadows.

It was now, at this hour, after tea, as the evening began to prowl slowly up the valley, that the fears came back. They were watching and waiting, sharpening their nails, snickering to each other as they planned their next snatch. And now, as he lay on his bed and watched the light through the window, cochineal imperceptibly stirring into gold, another thought struck him. What would happen to him if Rufus fell ill and wasn't able to give him the Sleeping Draught? Worse, still, what was going to happen next month when Rufus went away to school?

43

Tears welled up again, tears that the grownups said a soldier's son should be ashamed of, and should be teased out of him until the reservoirs ran dry (mind you, they didn't like bumptiousness either, and would knock that out of you too if the faintest shoot of it appeared in that unlikely climate).

So he wept some more, and as he wept, he thought of his father who he hardly knew but felt might understand because he had once or twice turned up in the last couple of years, and made distant friendly noises. Perhaps he would have told his father about the Frights.

But his father was far away at the moment doing secret things (nobody ever knew exactly what but they talked about it in lowered voices) with Intelligence, and the last time he had come home on leave, he hadn't seemed at all to be the person Adam remembered — turned now into a pale, withdrawn brooder with smudges of tiredness under his eyes, and a gift for getting on their Mother's nerves.

So his father couldn't be relied on, and the Germans seemed to be winning the war (with a thrust, so Rufus said, into the heart of the Corkses) and he, Adam, was going to be burgled by creatures that made the Reverend Biddle's description of the fiends of Hell sound like Three Little Piggies, and all the grownups could do was worry about figs.

It was all, he couldn't help thinking (with that sentience which, years after, makes one realize one was adult from the age of three), rather too much for a small boy to cope with.

If there were a Friend for little children above the bright blue sky, he could only suppose the Flying Fortresses were getting in His light.

9

In the courtyard of the stable-block, a couple of hundred yards from the big house, in the evening light, Franco Cattaneo was sitting at his easel painting his wife Griselda, who was wearing a pretty light-blue summer dress and an expression of wistfulness.

Old Mrs Sanderson had let them live in the flat above the stables because Franco had been a friend of her late husband's, and because she liked to feel that Cutcombe, as well as having its own milk, cream, butter, eggs, vegetables and fruit, now had its own resident artist as well. She also liked to think she had him exactly where she wanted him because, being Italian, though domiciled in London for several years and married to an English wife, he would have been interned as an alien had someone not sponsored him.

Franco himself was a saturnine man of robust appetites and a tongue second only to Granny Sanderson in the mordancy stakes, and since he was a good artist, particularly of landscape, and able to work wherever he found himself, he found Cutcombe and its curious denizens tolerably congenial, or at least as congenial as anything could be with Italy in the hands of preposterous assassins.

It was different for Griselda. The daughter of a small-time squire in Northamptonshire, brought up in a small-time Elizabethan manor-house next door to a handsome church, she had nursed an ambition for Life as magnificent and high-flying as the weathercock on the Late Perpendicular spire. It was Life that had led her to Franco, a creature so vital, so unpredictable, so intense. It was Life that had lured her from the dull confines of the Manor with its endless quagmire of trivialities and conversations with aunts, to the artistic and quasi-artistic purlieus of the Chelsea College of Art. True, she had been renounced by her family when she married Franco (she had met him after one of his raffish lectures and had been so swept off her feet that, for the first three months of their relationship, she had spent very little time off her back).

'That's what comes of bloody arty-crafty bloody fol-de-rol carryings-on,' her father had said pucely to his crumpet-faced wife. 'I bloody told you so. You should never have let her go off like that. Art School! Faugh. Lot of bloody fairies the lot of them.'

'Whatever else Franco is, Humphrey, and there are a great number of disagreeable things one could enumerate, fairy he most certainly is not. The man is by all accounts a satyr.'

'Don't quibble, Matilda. I know *he's* not a fairy. He's the exception that proves the rule, bloody making up for all the bloody rest of them. Even so, I wouldn't have minded if he was an Englishman. The family could do with some vigorous stock. And we had an artist on my mother's side in 1820 did some bloody fine racehorses. See 'em in the morning-room. But a Giovanni . . . An ice-creamer . . . It's really too bloody frightful for words. Anyway, I won't have her or her gigolo in the house. She's made her bed and now she must lie in it.'

Griselda had made her bed and now she was kicking vigorously at the sheets. She had confused Life with Art.

She didn't mind living in a little flat smelling only on certain days of manure, but she did object to the relentless self-absorption of the Artist. She had equated his early passion with an interest in herself, not realizing that the artist carries passion round with him as other people carry a bag of golfclubs: you simply can't play the game without it. And though she still found her husband witty, vital and inventive, her affection was breaking up on the granite of his egotism. She thought of herself as a gentle warm-hearted girl, indeed she was a gentle warm-hearted girl (though not quite as gentle and warm-hearted as she made out), spawned by heaven knew what quirk of genetic eccentricity by those Midland ironclads, but somewhere in her depths she had iron too, and she was damned if she was going to sit around for ever with this giant hogweed of an artist cutting off her light.

What she needed, perhaps, was someone like Tristram Sanderson.

They had first met before the war, before she and Franco had come down to Cutcombe, at a party somewhere in Chelsea, and they had talked easily and with a beguiling sense of rapport.

He seemed to represent the ideal synthesis of the country-man and the romantic hero with his cleanly-chiselled Rupert Brooke features, his degree in Modern Languages, and his ability to bag a brace of partridge seemingly with one barrel of a peashooter, to say nothing of the godlike way he bestrode his hunter. How her parents would have fawned on him, not that that should really have been a consideration, but it would be nice not to have to smell dung every time the wind was in the northwest.

Of course, Tristram wasn't really quite what he seemed, when she got to know him better, but then who was? She felt more for him now; more but different. What a pity emotions were never completely cut and dried. If she were in love with Tristram, why was Franco so difficult to leave?

Franco knew the answer.

'So, Zelda, you are thinking naughty.'

'Not at all. I was wondering what to do about dinner. All we have is a cabbage. And potatoes. It looks like bubble and squeak. Oh, and I've got a little corned beef.'

'Bubble and squeef.'

Griselda tried not to smile.

'Don't think naughty. It gives you lines. Here.'

He jabbed a stubby finger at the canvas.

'Naughty lines,' he continued. 'I try to paint a picture, Zelda, a picture of innocence. You are meant to look like a maid, a pure woman, casta, casta, my Zelda, a shepherdess, and all you do is look like a woman of Shepherd's Market, a mulier impudica, Zelda, you know what that means?'

She knew. Franco had been for one unlikely year in his youth a student for the priesthood at a seminary in Bologna. The only thing it seemed to have done for him was to accentuate the Catholic's tendency to believe that, if you confess everything, you can do anything; and to encourage a habit of peppering his conversation with dog-Latin. How rude and typical of him to say she looked like a dog-Latin whore when all she had been doing was recalling their love-making that morning.

'Ah, you are cruel, Zelda. You do not indulge the artist. You frown at me now. You make the mouth so. Try to fix your thoughts on nothing. Nothing, Zelda. That should be easy for you. I try to make it easy for you, you try to make it easy for me.'

'I do make it easy for you, Franco. Sometimes I think I make it too easy. It's always been the same, right from the beginning. You wanted to live with me. I lived with you. I didn't make you come and explain to my mother.'

'She has a face like a crumpet. La Crumpetta. I butter her up, yes?'

'It's all very well to make a joke of it now, but you didn't at the time. You ducked out of it. You just assumed I'd see to it myself. Just as you assumed I'd come down and bury myself with you here.'

'Ecco, ecco. Now she gives me the story, eh? Etchetera. Etchetera.'

'I cook, I clean, I wash, I make the bed . . . ' really, she knew, she was going about this all wrong, but once roused, she never let common sense come between her and her emotions. He'd slighted her, damn it. She'd had just about all of him she could take.

'Yes, Zelda, it is true. You wait on me tooth and claw.'

She collapsed with laughter while Franco waved a reproving brush at her.

'You think too much, Zelda, you give me the lines here, you give me the lines there. You English girls, you do not understand life like the Italian woman. You think while they act. It is the difference between your Jane Austen heroines, shall I do this, shall I do that, shall I think, shall I feel . . . and Petrarch's Laura. She *lives* . . . She . . . she *is*'

Griselda, who had seldom seen Franco touch a book, expressed the opinion that it was probably nothing to do with nationalities, but simply that one had been written by a woman while the other was an idealized portrait by a man, and further that Franco had never read a single page of Jane Austen or Petrarch for that matter. She was gratified when he acknowledged the fact with a little grimace.

'I have read *about* it,' he said vaguely waving his hands, 'And anyway, why bother with mere words? I take it in with the eyes, with the pores. I have seen the Italian women. I know. From the principessa to the little whores on the Corso, they vibrate with life as Italy herself vibrates with life . . . '

'If you like it so much, why don't you go back there?' Unfair, of course, but really.

'Do not be ridiculous, Zelda. You know very well. There are certain difficulties in time of war. Besides, I cannot work there. I am a prophet without honour. This is my home now for my work, even though I am kept here in the country like a criminal.'

Griselda decided to change the subject. The sun was oppressive in the stable-yard and the dung from Rodgers's midden was playing a ripe olfactory capriccio which grew by the minute more virulent. It was too hot to be heated, and she knew she'd have to sit for another half hour at least.

'Anyway,' she said, 'about dinner . . .'

Ah,' said Franco triumphantly, seizing upon the opportunity, 'what I say. You English . . . no soul. You are not spirituosa, Zelda. Do you think when Leonardo paint La Gioconda she was dreaming about cabbages? Do you imagine she thinking about bubble and squeak, that is why she has an expression so mysterious? Do you think she say to herself "I am always hearing about this zuppa inglese of cabbage and potatoes and it sound so wizard I am going to give it to the old man instead of tagliatelle tonight." Eh?'

But Griselda had gone back to thinking about Tristram again, though this time she was careful not to put any lines where Franco might notice them.

She remembered how Tristram had joked about their names.

'We're a couple of heroes,' he said, 'Tristram and Griselda . . . it's the very fabric of Romance, give or take a syllable. If Marie de France were around she'd make us into a Lay, though I'm not sure her presence would be necessarily welcome.'

Griselda had blushed pleasantly, and started into the usual explanation of her name.

'It means Grey Maid of Battle,' she said. 'No one quite knows why I was given the name. I mean, it's not like me and it certainly isn't like my parents. I can't help feeling someone else's Godparent must have crashed the christening.'

'Mine's typical Mother, I'm afraid. She was convinced I was going to turn into something titanic. The Son of Cutcombe had to be the best . . . like the gooseberries.'

Taking care not to throw her features out of kilter, she gave a semi-quaver of a sigh and thought how much she really and truly wanted to see him again. As if in a measure of response to her thoughts, his son Rufus put his narrow white face round the corner of the gate.

'I've had my tea,' he announced. 'Adam has been sent to his room.'

50

'Ah,' said Franco, 'the seedy one. Ecce homunculus candidus. Come here and I will put some colour in your cheeks,' and he advanced on the little boy waving his brush extravagantly.

Rufus retreated behind Griselda, and a steeplechase ensued in which Franco emerged the victor, pinning Rufus between his knees and darting the brush at him like an enraged Stuka.

'No,' yelled Rufus, 'pax. They'll send me to my room too if I get covered with that muck.'

'Muck?' shouted Franco in mock aghast, 'muck? You call the material of Titian by this Anglo-Saxon four-letter word?'

'Don't, Franco,' pleaded Griselda. 'You're always getting them into trouble. Anyway, I thought you wanted to finish the picture. Come back later, Rufus, and I'll give you some bubble and squeak.'

'You certainly know how to tempt a man,' said Franco, releasing the child. 'What you want here anyway, cream-faced loon?'

He had once done a series of Shakespearean set designs (never used).

Rufus whispered urgently in his ear, and Franco, selecting a small bottle of distilled water from his box, handed it over to him.

'Only one drop, remember,' said Franco with an apothecary's scrupulousness.

Rufus nodded and scudded off again like a rabbit across the cobbled court.

'What on earth are you up to,' said Griselda, vaguely, 'always egging them on? You're more of a child than they are.'

The day's sun and the argument had given her a slight headache. She wanted to go in. 'All men are little boys at heart,' said Franco, 'and all little girls are women.'

'But serously,' she protested, not really interested.

'Nothing, Zelda, nothing,' said Franco, suddenly assuaging her. 'Just a little game we're playing.'

51

10

Lieutenant Thomas Lippincott was in love — a description
that he himself would have regarded as too tentative. He
would have preferred to describe it as a tragic madness not
dissimilar from Hippolytus's love for Phaedra but without
the nasty incest motif. Alternatively, he might have told
you (if he had known you well) that a mighty flood of pure
emotion, making Alph the Sacred River look like Minehead Town effluent, coursed through his veins making it
difficult to pee in the mornings and totally circumscribing
his horizons.

He was a man somewhat given to romantic hyperboles,
possibly as a result of short-sightedness and a reluctance to
wear glasses, but saved from excess by a self-deprecating
humour that drew its source from some ancestral fund of New
England practicality. Indeed, though his only close relative
was a distant father (his mother had died when he was a
child), his family was one of the oldest in Massachusetts.

He had, in fact, been a reasonably well-balanced
character up till twelve months ago.

Thomas's job as Education Officer at the St Paget's Bay
Gunnery Base, five miles down the road from Cutcombe
situated on a stretch of coast notable for its red cliffs and
glutinous sand, might not have seemed, on the face of it,
unduly deranging for an intelligent young man. And indeed
only a year before he had still been at MIT, happily working on the putative behaviour of sub-atomic particles.

He had been diverted from this area of elegant and
momentous tininess by an instruction from his professor to
join a reactor project at Columbia which initially aroused
curiosity but which increasingly made him feel first embarrassed, then alarmed and ultimately deeply disturbed — a

project inevitably leading, he could discern, to the capacity for destruction of the nuclear force itself — a project that came to be included under the general title of Manhattan.

He vividly (too vividly) remembered the whole episode, particularly the morning when his predicament had first come home to him.

He had just been running through some figures when the Head of Project came by with some officials, an unusual event since the whole building was by then Top Security and any kind of visitor was as rare as a crested hoopoe. He recognized one of them, a glassy- (some said twinkly-)eyed Bostonian called Vannevar Bush, known to be some kind of top Co-ordinator of activities such as this.

'Well, Lippincott,' said Bush, after introductions had been made, 'how are you geting along?'

'Yes, sir.'

'Yes, sir? What kind of answer is that?'

'Well, sir. It's these equations.'

'What equations, Lippincott?'

'Controlling the chain reaction, sir. I'm not too happy about certain implications . . . and what do we know about radiation effects?'

The officials exchanged glances. Lippincott's findings appeared to give them no particular cause for alarm.

'You leave the implications to us, Lippincott.'

And the party went on its way.

But he couldn't leave the implications to them. He knew there was a war on, and Hitler did indeed seem to be an archetype of all that he found appalling, but this . . . this seemed like war on life itself.

As he pondered on the somewhat (he felt) unsympathetic approach by his superiors to the possible destruction of the biosphere, he recalled the earlier news from Berkeley that a team of chemists had succeeded in isolating an artificial element that was far cheaper to produce than Uranium 235, but even more fissile. They had grimly, if suitably, named it after

53

the king of Hell — plutonium. Its significance lay in the fact that the government would now, of course, be planning the mass-production of fissile material without dependence on rare and consequently self-limiting sources outside the USA.

The realization left Lippincott feeling very disturbed indeed.

At this point, he had with considerable difficulty obtained permission to leave the project and join the Army. If he hadn't he was convinced that he would have become unhinged, since the implications of his researches daily became more and more horrifying. Even now, the memory of certain equations rose in his consciousness like bile. It seemed to him that he had collaborated on the ultimate desecration and that he was marked for life. It was as simple as that. Thank God, he had escaped — too late, of course, there were some things you could never leave behind — but distance helped. So did the pills a harassed doctor had prescribed for him on transit through New York.

'A mildly sedative effect,' he had explained. 'Take two a day and one at night. Next please.'

It was not surprising, now, that he should feel out of place giving the men their weekly lecture on current affairs and how not to get venereal disease in Bridgwater (a duty shared with an elusive Medical Officer), but the very mundanity of his activities he found comforting. Though huge and malign images haunted his day and preyed upon his dreams, he could keep despair at bay by concentrating on spirochaeta and crabs.

As for further education, on the whole it had to be said that the men were disinclined to receive any education at all, current or otherwise, while the officers positively questioned the very fons et origo of its purpose.

'Romeo, Romeo, wherefore art thou Romeo?' the buffalo-like Major Caldwell (to whom Thomas had once rashly confided his interest in poetry) would croon mincingly. 'You think that's gonna win the fuckin' war? I wandered lonely as a cloud? You try telling that to them Messerschmitt boys.'

'Yes, but.'

'Piping down the valleys wild? You think that's what they're doing down the Caucasus, you think that's the reason the Panzers are knocking shit out of them?'

'No, but.'

'You can keep your education till when the war's over and then you can keep it some more.'

Major Caldwell spoke with all the confidence of a man who would never have to unravel the eccentricity of the electron or speculate upon the Seventeenth Century World Picture: all Major Caldwell would have to do would be to lead his father's cattle regularly to the slaughterhouse and pick up a nice fat cheque which he could then spend sucking on country pleasures and snorting in the Seven Sleepers' Den until such time as it pleased his Maker to drive Major Chuck himself to the quiet slaughterhouse of his bedroom, where he would yield up his divine spark with the same uncomprehending bovinity as his beasts. Unless, of course, the war in some way interrupted his easy run, as Thomas had just the faintest inkling that it could, a sort of half-seen intimation of something that suggested blood.

Perhaps it was simply the aura of slaughterhouse about the man, but Thomas felt not. He had had these cloudy presentiments many times in the past, maybe encouraged by his literary and metaphysical leanings, or perhaps the occasioning of them, that things not so much had happened before, but were happening somewhere very close, just around the corner as it were, simultaneously.

It was a sensation difficult to pinpoint, but the nearest he could get was to liken it to picking up Radio Free Albania when you were listening to the One O'Clock News. He would describe this only to people whose spirits he thought might be kindred (and there were few in West Somerset). As if ghosts, he would say, were not necessarily from the past but shadows from an alternative present. He never mentioned these matters at all to Major Chuck, sensing his reaction would be unconstructive.

But to Thomas these considerations, at a time of strain, loneliness, boredom, disruption and danger, made life infinitely more exhilarating. Man's view of Time existed simply to keep him in, like a wall round a children's playground, but it certainly wouldn't be God's conception of it, or even an enlightened observer's, he thought. And as at the Cutcombe lunch, he would amuse himself with imagining all the eventualities that might develop from every pregnant moment.

One paper he had recently come across even suggested that it might be possible, under certain conditions, to cross from one parallel state to another. Which could get curiouser and curiouser, thought Thomas, as long as you could get back to the one you started in.

Because, he had to admit it, when all the speculations were over, what he really wanted to do was get back to young Mrs Sanderson.

It had happened while he was out on his push-bicycle. He had bought an ancient Hudson from the local store and, when he discovered that his duties at the Camp involved little more than arranging a twice-weekly film show at the cinema, revising the current affairs lecture, and briefing newcomers on the Camp and its environs, he had embarked on extensive explorations of the countryside.

West Somerset in high summer gave him inexhaustible pleasure. As well as being heavy with the scent of meadowsweet, angelica, lime, honeysuckle, jasmine and clustering rose from a myriad cottage gardens, tinged intermittently with more pungent odours of wild garlic, devil's stink-horn and sometimes even fox, the very air was redolent of poetry. Coleridge and Wordsworth had passed this way, along with the Person from Porlock who had disturbed the Kubla Khan.

He had even considered doing a little local research while he was down here, to find out, maybe, who the Person from Porlock was — not perhaps a random visitor but a jealous local poet out to wreck Coleridge's already tenuous powers of concentration. In the English country, he knew, a well-timed visit can do more harm to the sensitive soul than blocked drains.

At other times, the very beauty of the scene would react upon the blight within him (hidden away, carefully covered, but always ready to break out) and he would see the banks charred and dead, everything wiped out — Coleridge, Porlock, Somerset, the sweets of civilization, the glory that was Greece, laughter and literature, fullness of lip and gentleness of brow, in a moment, in the twinkling of an eye, at the last trumpet.

And then he would pedal on again, leaving the dark thoughts behind like the fat flies that bobbed about in his wake as he toiled through deliciously named villages — Combe Sydenham, Huish Blanchflower, Clatworthy — where time seemed to hang immobile, as if they were sited on the very lip of a Black Hole instead of the cidery slopes of the Brendons — and panted up luscious dank fern-smelling high-backed lanes to summits of commons where the breeze would lick his brow and the distant sea danced for him sedately below, a vision of broad blue bombazine, well-washed if scantly ironed.

Major Caldwell had, it was true, taken him to task about his frequent absences from the Camp.

'I kinda get the feeling, Lippincott, that you're not pulling your weight in this war. This war is not a ramble through briar-strewn country lanes with a book in your bag and a lupin up your ass. This war is ugly, and shitty, Lippincott. Remember that the human body is soft, Lippincott. That is why we have to make our minds hard. You, as Education Officer, above all should bear that in mind. I want your report in three days' time on a Mind-Hardening Course for the men.'

'Local topography is very much part of my brief, Major. I assure you I get no pleasure out of it. I detest bicycling. I'd

57

rather not have to go out bicycling today, Major, if you don't mind. I'd rather get down to some mind-strengthening with the men. I know they'd enjoy it. And it'd prove how useful Education is.'

'No, uh, Lippincott. I guess you'd better carry on with your project. Ride hard. And for Chrissake be military. If you've gotta get down and have a shit, shit briskly. That will be all.'

It was on one of these expeditions that he had stopped to buy a soothing draught. He was so hot he didn't mind what came to hand − ale, blushful hippocrene or, as it turned out, fizzy lemonade. It was not ice-cold. It was not even cold. It was lukewarm, English-style, but it seemed to do the trick, and he was burping quietly and preparing to hand the bottle back to the old lady who kept the store, when a vision entered his life. It seemed, when he could find words to describe it, to take the form of a young woman in a small Morris car, and who appeared to be in something of a hurry.

She stopped in the middle of the narrow street, and got out, approaching him in the manner of one who is going to ask a yokel to hold the reins.

'Watch out for my car, would you, in case something comes?' she said. 'I simply can't find anywhere to park.'

He did not point out that she had made absolutely no discernible effort to find anywhere to park, nor did he realize that she had spied him from a distance and simply collected him as she collected, effortlessly, anyone who looked as though they might be amusing.

He mumbled words of service and obligingness and she disappeared into the muggy interior of the store.

At this point, a tractor came round the bend behind him, and stopped.

Thomas didn't even notice it. He felt that the world, having been for as long as he could remember black and white, was suddenly bathed in colour. She was the most beautiful, the most exquisite creature he had ever seen in his life.

58

The tractor heaved and bubbled patiently, like an elephant digesting spinach.

Thomas at length became aware of its presence.

'Sorry,' he said to its ratty-capped, swarthy-featured driver. 'She'll be out in a minute.'

'Zum folk got all the time. You from 'merica?'

'That's right.'

Thomas sensed the imminence of a catechism, and did his best to look unforthcoming. He didn't want to discuss his antecedents. He simply wanted to know who she was.

'This car.'

'Little Morris.'

'Do you know it? Do you know whose it is?'

'Course I knows it. I work for un, don't I? Leastways for her ma-in-law. I be cowman.'

'Where . . . tell me . . . where does she live? What's her name?'

'What's it to you, mister? Lot of funny people about these days. Careless talk costs lives, don't it? Keep mum, that's what they say.'

There had been a scare recently about a spy in the area, and Thomas had already stumbled across the villagers' wariness of strangers. They talked about the people across the hill as 'foreigners'. He felt it best to be open with the man.

'I'm in love with her.'

The cowman, it was Rodgers, burst into laughter, showing a set of strong brown teeth.

Thomas was momentarily offended.

'Have I said something funny?'

The cowman shook his head, wiping tears from his eyes.

'Mebbe you have, mebbe you haven't. Better know what you'm up against, that be all. Better know the nature of the affliction. That be Mrs Sanderson, that be. Young Mrs Sanderson. Two boys her got, husband in the military in Lunnon, and a lot of admiration in these parts. Very popular lady be Mrs Sanderson.'

At that moment the subject of their discussion came out of the shop.

'Oh. Sorry, Rodgers.'

'That be all right, missus.'

If she was interested in Thomas, she was doing a superb job in not showing it. She looked at him (she had found this extraordinarily effective in the past) with as much passing interest as if he were a bluebottle.

'Oh . . . Thank you er'.

'Lippincott. Lieutenant Thomas Lippincott, ma'am,' and he added because he had seen it done in films, 'At your service.'

'Thank you, Mr Lippincott. I don't think I shall be needing any more service just at present. But thank you for holding my horse, I mean car.'

Thomas's mind raced, although he sensed its rate of acceleration would hardly have done credit to Stephenson's Rocket. Delving desperately into his bicycle bag, he withdrew a large Hershey bar which he had been saving for his lunch, and thrust it into her hands. She looked at it as if it might contain a vileness.

'For your sons,' he babbled.

Comprehension flooded across her face like a glorious sunset. She smiled at him so wonderfully he nearly let go of his handlebars.

'How sweet of you,' she said.

'Not at all.'

He was conscious of Rodgers watching with a knowing twinkle in his roving eye.

'Sweets to the sweet,' he was going to say but thought it might be impertinent at such an early stage of their acquaintance, and anyway hardly original, stopped, blushed, and watched, relieved that she had not noticed his embarrassment but aghast at her departure, as she slipped the little Morris into gear, and drove off at a pace which would have astonished its designers with a ferrety squeal of tyres.

'Too kind,' trailed on the wind like chiffon.

'Hey wait I was going to ask . . . ' but she was gone.

'You'm better off with the little tarts down Watchet way, they don't call it Watchet for nothing,' Rodgers added cryptically, but Thomas was too elated and disturbed to investigate the allegation.

'Where does she live?'

'Up the lane, first left to Combe Withiel and then take the driveway on the right up through the woods. But don't say I told 'ee. More'n my life's worth.'

Thomas promised to be circumspect.

'Don't think her minds about that,' replied the cowman, 'But whatever it is 'ee do, 'ee won't cut no ice with 'er unless you got summat amazing special. Whole county's arter Mrs Sanderson from Lord Lieutenant down.'

11

All that was five weeks ago, five weeks and three days to be relentlessly accurate, but it was as vivid to Thomas as if it were this morning as he trudged disconsolately down through the woods towards the house on his way back from a long and solitary and, yes, sulky trudge (because of her attention to the slaughtering Major) upon which he had embarked after lunch.

The object of his passion did not mind his sulk, in fact it rather amused her, and he knew it. He realized he was a trifle serious for her taste, and he had come to terms with the fact, always difficult for the romantically-minded, that he himself did not match up to the classic delineations of the romantic hero. He was of medium height, with medium-coloured hair, and a medium cast of profile. He had a medium if diffident charm of which he was modestly aware, but nobody could, or did, call him an Adonis.

The other thing was, he was convinced that she was playing him and the Major off against each other.

The thought was bitter to him as he crossed the little bridge over the stream and caught sight of the house winking palely between the trees, and he felt a curious sense of emptiness. Even the birds seemed to have flown from this part of the woods except, he noticed, an old robin that looked at him with eyes full of an immemorial prescience. He remembered a story of Algernon Blackwood's about the Trod, the green road along the moors where, if you set foot, you were carried away by beautiful laughing evil people and were never seen again, and momentarily quickened his pace. But a few steps more, and he could hear the generator that provided the power for the house, a temperamental minor deity tended by Rodgers and appeased with dead mice, thumping in its oily sanctum beside the garage.

It was still very hot in the woods. The humid vegetable warmth reminded him of a trip he had once taken with his father to the Everglades, and he was comforting himself with the thought that at least they didn't have alligators here when a sudden large stirring in the undergrowth brought his heart up in one bound to nestle against the tip of his uvula.

'Whaat?' he quavered. 'Who's that? Come out!'

A small figure disengaged itself from the saplings and presented itself on the path.

'I caught you with my anti-tank gun, so your track's off. At least.'

It was Rufus, the elder boy, her elder boy. Thomas found him, he had to confess, an eerie creature but addressed himself to him pleasantly for her sake, stifling an instinct to garotte.

'I surrender,' he said, his syllables forcing a passageway through his left ventricle.

'Good. What is your mission?'

'I come in peace.'

'That's cowboys and Indians.'

Rufus's face expressed the utmost disgust.

'Talk German or I'll have to wipe you out.'

'Very vell, zen. Mein Führer haf ordered me here to bring ein invitation for ein pardy at mein campf. Your mutter has not tell you? Ja?'

'Invitation? What sort of party?'

'You know ze sort of sing. Tanzen and trinken. Bier and schnapps and fizzilimonad, und frankfurters and hamburgers und hot schweinhunds . . . und, und bratwurst for ze liddle brats . . . und . . . '

'How boring.'

'Ja, das ist boring. Ve like to haf ze boring pardies. Zat vay ve get at ze English to fall asleep so how you say ve catch zem napping.'

'That's silly.'

Thomas restrained himself with difficulty from giving the little brat a clip round the ear, and tried to think of him as the fruit of his mother's loins. Finally he gave up and, as the silence began to be oppressive, he selected another topic.

'Where's Adam?'

On slender acquaintance he had grown fond of the younger child who, he thought, seemed to inhabit a more painful universe than his brother — a universe of which Thomas, with passion unassuaged and jealousy surging dangerously past the critical mark, was now an honorary citizen.

'Adam was sent to his room. Why does everyone bother about Adam? Adam's a weed. He wants an Armistice. Adam's a traitor.'

This seemed to be pitching it a trifle strong, but Thomas felt it might not be the moment to go into the pros and cons of pacifism, and politely disengaged himself expressing the wish that hostilities might reach a satisfactory conclusion for all parties.

'You've just walked over a minefield so your entire

column's in smithereens,' said Rufus, as he walked away.

Later, when Thomas found the mother in the drawing-room pouring her pre-prandial gin and tonic (he noticed the gin looked suspiciously like the stuff they carried in the base, and surmised that Major Chuck must've been playing the large-hearted American again), he did venture the opinion that Adam might need rather special handling.

'He's a sensitive child.'

'Oh, I don't know. It's not as bad as all that.'

The mother sat down and crossed her legs with a sleek swishy sound that betokened silk stockings and silk under-wear (where did they come from? Who were they for? Major Chuck's big hand again?) that betokened unbeliev-able hinterlands of pleasure. Thomas almost fainted.

'Speak roughly to your little boy,' she continued, making her buttocks perfectly comfortable, 'and beat him when he sneezes. For he can thoroughly enjoy the pepper when he pleases.'

The rhyme, Thomas had noticed, was much employed by the family.

'Yes . . . but . . . he's only six.'

'Are you trying to tell me . . . ' the mother seldom became cross, she disliked the waste of energy involved, but when she did she became very cross indeed, 'are you trying to tell me how to look after my own son? Go on, admit it. You are. Funny people coming here trying to tell us how to look after our own sons. Shoo. Go away. Horrid little man.'

'But I'm only . . . '

'Only? Only what? You're only here to amuse me.' Her rage abated as quickly as it had arisen. 'That's what you must never forget, Mr Lippincott. Don't get ideas above your station. And, talking of your station, tell me more about the party. Are you asking Franco and what's her name?'

She had never really cared for Franco's wife, though in fairness to her, this was nothing to do with Griselda's affair with her husband (which she neither knew nor would have

64

wished to know about — his fall from grace being of a much more serious nature).

She simply thought of the girl as being fey, rather silly, up in the air all the time, a bit of a tit.

'I'm not so sure about Franco. Isn't he an alien and supposed to be restricted or something? Or something?'

'Oh, don't be so stuffy, Thomas. Really, you people. There's such a thing as trust. That's the trouble with you Americans. You have no instinct for things. That's why you have to spell everything out.'

Unfair though he felt this was in his particular case, Thomas couldn't help thinking she had hit Major Chuck right on the head. But why, then, did she keep on seeing him? And why did she have to keep crossing her legs like that?

Her attention seemed to be wandering. Was she bored with him? What did he see in her anyway, a beautiful vessel certainly, but undeniably empty! And then suddenly her eyes swept down on his like kestrels, wild like amatory Assyrians, like . . . but the moment was too strong for simile. At last he knew, without the slightest jot, tittle or scintilla of a doubt, that sooner or later, and it looked like sooner, all his despairs were going to be allayed.

There was a pause.

Outside, the woods wandered away into the shadows on the flank of Cutcombe Hill. The evening star came out, a red stag lifted his antlers and sniffed the faint breeze which, for the first time that day, stirred the great oaks along the edge of Luxborough Forest, and a barn owl essayed an early reconnaissance, patrolling for field mice along Six Acre hedgerow. Further away, touched by the sun's declining rays, men were killing each other, nation pounced on nation, pogroms were unleashed, cities blazed, tyrants pontificated and blood flowed like the Severn Bore. But everything beyond those four walls seemed to Thomas as he sat there to be part of some other universe, the red earth, the screams of fieldmice, an alien matter, nothing to do with him at all. There was only one evening star for him, and she was sitting in front of him letting him look up the furthest galactic reaches of her frock.

Suddenly she stood up, arbitarily withdrawing the privilege. He didn't know where to look. There seemed nothing else worth looking at.

'Come along, Thomas. I think you'd better come down to the summerhouse. I've got something to show you.'

He wondered afterwards whether she would or would not have shown him the ultimately interesting something down in the summerhouse at that precise stage in their relationship. Probably not, he reflected later, knowing her dislike of wasting a carrot on a willing donkey. But anyway, he was not to discover, for just at that moment, as all he had ever dreamed of seemed to be about to be unleashed, a distant figure on the lawn outside shuffled dejectedly across his line of vision.

It was Adam, allowed up for a final half-hour before he went to bed again.

He presented such a picture of melancholy that Thomas, whose heart was considerably softer than his springs of life at that moment, experienced only a brief inner turmoil before turning to her and shaking his head.

'I promised I'd go look at the kids' sailboats next time I came. They won't forgive me if I don't. Maybe I could see the summerhouse some other day?'

As it happened, though he wasn't to know it at the time, he couldn't have advanced his cause more effectively. Julia was piqued. People didn't refuse her. It was beyond the bounds of her conjecture. She gasped like a defenestrated goldfish and momentarily lost control of the situation.

'Really, Lieutenant,' was all she could say. 'Really, Lieutenant.'

Deciding that he must have taken leave of his senses, Thomas opened the French windows and strode manlily out onto greensward. He felt like that Older Adam vacating Eden.

Halfway up the great sweep of lawn that stretched for a couple of hundred yards up to the wall of the kitchen garden, another path branched off towards the woods. Following it, where it skirted a small pond, Thomas found the boy bleakly kicking twigs into the water.

'What's the matter?' said Thomas.

'Nothing,' said Adam.

'Come on,' said Thomas, 'I can't help if you don't tell me.'

'Nothing. Nothing.'

'Nothing shall come of nothing. Mend thy speech a little.'

Adam shrugged and set off again, striking deeper and deeper into the trees.

> 'Now came still evening on and twilight grey
> Had in her silver livery all things clad,
> Silence accompanied, and bird and beast,
> They to their grassy couch, these to their nest,
> Were slunk,'

said Thomas.

Adam padded stolidly forward.

'D'you often come out by yourself like this? Hm? What does he in the woods so late, a furlong from the castle gate?'

Adam was a polite little boy or else he would have told Thomas to go away. Instead he shot him a furious glance.

Thomas laughed.

'You wouldn't laugh if you knew who lived up there,' Adam said, pointing up the side of the hill to where the old quarry workings spilled tsunamis of shrub-crested slate-slag down across the head of the valley.

'Oh? Who *does* live up there?'

'In the thickest part there's a tunnel that goes miles into the hill. That's where they live. Rufus said so . . . ' A look of terror crossed the face. 'You won't tell, will you? I promised . . . '

'What on earth are you talking about?'

But try as he might, Thomas could get no more out of the little boy.

'It's my bedtime now. I've got to go back.'

Although it would not be dark outside for another couple of hours, it was gloomy under the wings of the trees. Somewhere far off, an owl called prematurely. Adam looked suddenly alarmed.

'Just then flew by a monstrous crow, as black as a tar barrel, which frightened both the heroes so, they quite forgot their quarrel.'

'I've got to go back now.'

They padded down the path together, the distant cooees of Nanny sounding like the squawks of an archaeopteryx.

'You're always saying things like that. And anyway we weren't quarrelling.'

'What things?'

'That monstrous crow. Have you ever seen a monstrous crow?'

'Can't say I have. It's from a poem.'

'I haven't either. But I think one of them's a monstrous owl.'

'What are you talking about, Adam?'

'I can't tell you. Sorry.'

Thomas felt a little irritated. Here he was, giving up heaven knew what delights, and all he got was veiled references.

'You're being very veiled this evening, Adam.'

'You'd be veiled too if you were . . . You'd be veiled if . . . ' his voice trailed away.

Adam couldn't really make Thomas out. He was chatty and interested and always saying things Adam didn't understand but wanted to. But the biggest thing he couldn't understand about him was that grownups were supposed to be unpleasant. Grownups had got it in for children. A timeless malevolent ordinance had decreed that if a grownup saw a child, he was duty-bound to take the stuffing out of it and generally give it a bad time. Any tendency towards bumptiousness must be sat on, any weakness mocked, any sensitivity denigrated, any fear played upon after the manner of Chelly-Chops, ruthlessly skewering Scarlatti on the spinet.

Exactly why grownups felt like this, Adam could not understand. He did not wish them any harm. He didn't want to comment on their exceedingly boring conversation, or to stop them eating Cutcombe clotted cream because it would make them sick, or to urge them to romp in manly manner and on the other hand to nag because they got their clothes dirty. He was quite prepared to leave them alone if only they would do the same for him. But no, they weren't happy unless they'd got their knife into you.

He remembered when his mother was very ill, well fairly ill, in those days when he still placed some measure of confidence in her. He used to loiter outside her door, and someone, he could never remember who, someone had said just in passing, with mocking voice, 'What's the matter, little boy? D'you think she's going to die?' That, of course, was exactly what he had thought, and he thought it still more after that.

There were other things about grownups he didn't comprehend. Why, for instance, when they seemed to have a limitless supply of chocolates in that box on top of the cupboard in the library, didn't they eat chocolates all day?

He would have to ask Thomas because, yes, even though he was a grownup, even though he didn't eat chocolates all day long, Thomas was different.

'Is something bothering you, Adam?'

It was clear the child had something on his mind. Was it merely the byproduct of the English country-house war on children, or something more esoteric? He tried another approach.

'This monstrous owl of yours. How monstrous is it?'

'It's monstrous, all right.'

'But owls don't get to be very monstrous.'

'Nor do crows.'

'Thomas had to admit that this was true.

'Even so,' he pressed ahead, 'your owl's pretty big. As big as me?'

The little boy nodded.

'Just as big as you. In fact, it's more like a man.'

'Where did you see it?'

'In my mind.'

Thomas felt like laughing. The child obviously suffered from nightmares. At this moment, however, the elder brother rounded a corner and came hurrying towards them.

'Don't say anything,' whispered Adam, urgently.

'But . . . '

'Don't say anything. Please.'

'Where've you been?' said Rufus, his pinched little gaze ferreting about between them. 'Nanny's in a frightful wax. It's time for your bath.'

'I'm afraid it's my fault,' said Thomas, 'I asked Adam to show me where you have these boat-races.'

Rufus gave them another sharper glance as though expecting amplification, but Thomas said no more, sensing the younger brother, tense as a barrage balloon in a high wind, trembling beside him. And later, standing on the front steps of Cutcombe House, as he confronted a bristling Nanny whose breasts under her striped uniform dress, normally so cornucopic, now pointed accusingly at him, he explained again that the delay had been entirely occasioned by himself.

'Adam is guiltless,' he told her puckishly, 'free from blame. He walketh undefiled in the way. Adam before the Fall. No Sin,' he added, noticing her eyes bulge. 'Personally, of course, I have always inclined to the Nestorian if not the Pelagian School.'

'I don't know about that I'm sure, but he's a very naughty little boy for not telling you he had to be back which he very well knows. Nothing but trouble you are,' she addressed herself to Adam. 'You'll be late for yesterday next. Run along now. Sharp's the word and quick's the action.'

Nanny had picked up a useful vocabulary of starchy phrases from Nanny Fairfax who looked after the children over at Combe Huish, but she still found them sitting a little awkwardly on her tongue, and now she slipped into a riper vernacular.

'I ran your bath quarter hour back, so 'ee'll just have to have it lukewarm. No more hot water now. It'll learn 'ee to be late.'

Adam wondered who Luke was and why he should have had this curious taste for tepid baths, and why Nanny was in such a hurry tonight, and whether Rufus was going to punish him.

Nanny wondered whether Rodgers would still be waiting in the musty twilight of the stables, those terrible swift hands of his at the ready, ready to tear the buttons off her uniform, claw with delicious clumsiness at her bodice, and, suddenly and wonderfully sensitive, play the Flight of the Bumblebee on her gusset.

Thomas wondered whether Julia would still be in the drawing-room and, if she were, whether she would feel inclined to re-issue the invitation he had so fecklessly refused.

Rufus wondered whether Adam had said anything to the American. He hadn't liked the look on their faces when he came round the corner.

But all their speculations were interrupted by the sudden appearance of Mother herself.

'Really,' she said, addressing the children but including everyone in her disfavour, 'You shouldn't be down here at this hour of the evening. Up to the Nursery at once, both of you. Really, Nanny,' she switched her flashing eyes in the

71

direction of the unfortunate melons, 'really. We can't have children charging all over the house after tea. I thought I had made that quite clear.'

Nanny looked considerably put out, but Thomas once again sprang to the rescue.

'It's my fault, I'm afraid, I . . . '

Julia cut him short.

'Goodness,' she said sweetly, 'I thought you'd gone hours ago. Shouldn't you be helping win the war or something?'

12

Tristram woke, after what seemed like many hours of sleep, with those unpleasant sensations of doom which so often attend the return of consciousness, but which usually have no foundation. In fact on this occasion, however, he was aware that the situation was worse than intimation. He was in trouble. No doubt the Gestapo officer would return shortly and demand information which the Son of Cutcombe was honour-bound to withhold. (Even as the thought crossed his mind, a guard, noticing him wake, pressed a buzzer on the desk.)

He wondered which part of his body they would start on first. Nonetheless, since there seemed to be no point in dwelling on the unpleasant, he began to speculate on the possibility of escape. It seemed more manly.

The room he lay in was bare. Just a truckle bed, a couple of chairs, a desk, and the regulation bare bulb hanging from a flaking white ceiling.

Behind the table, a window loosely boarded from without, showed slivers of a now-tranquil sky fading into twilight behind a Nissen hut with, beyond, a glimpse of a field and the corner of a small wood.

It might be just possible, he decided, to make a break for it, and frankly he saw no other possibility. If he stayed where he was they would doubtless torture him and then shoot him like a dog — not that he had ever seen a dog shot but he understood it was done without compunction.

He was relieved to find that the knot which had been in his stomach for months now, a knot that had lodged and grown like a monstrous foetus through the training, the terrible jumps and the more and more rigorous exercises, was beginning miraculously to unravel. Now that action was at hand, he felt, though unpredecentedly peculiar, clear of eye and keen of limb.

However, since there seemed to be no possibility of action just at this minute, the guard with the gun still looming large, he let his mind turn to the fount of his troubles. How had he got into all this?

He thought of Cutcombe, so far away, so green, so full of possibility and yet so addled by his mother and her ambition for him to be her beloved son in whom she was well pleased, so blighted by her ability to stir up guilt in him. It was his fear of failing her that had made it impossible for him to do anything but win.

It was she who had master-minded him into his First Eleven cap a year before anyone else in the history of the School. It was she who had browbeaten the President of Trinity to admit him even though he was down for Balliol. It was she who had wheedled the general to get him into the Rifle Brigade at the start of the war, and from thence into Intelligence because she thought it would be safer. (She had been wrong about that, though, hadn't she?)

It was she, even, who had teed him up into securing his wife.

Mother had wanted it. Mother had indicated that only

the catch of the County would be good enough for the Son of Cutcombe, but she'd slipped up on that too, because the catch of the County had turned out to be nothing but a high-class cocotte.

Even that wouldn't have mattered if it hadn't been wartime. But the endless stretches of day after day in bleak top-security camps – he had been seconded to special duties when it was discovered that he spoke French fluently (thanks to his mother's insistence on a French governess in early youth) – finding himself far from his friends, on desolate woldy stretches of Lincolnshire among (for some reason) Dutchmen in whose conversation and impenetrable language one could hunt for enlightenment as diligently and with as little success as an alchemist in pursuit of the magisterium; all this had occasioned boredom, loneliness, depression and, in the end, despair. There was no end to it, no goal in sight, only the light fading in the tunnel behind him.

And then, of course, there was the jumping.

He remembered the first parachute training-course he had attended. They hadn't told him at this stage about his role with the Resistance. He hadn't yet embarked on the endless questions and answers, the topographical tutorials, the survival training, the unarmed combat, the assimilation of a totally new personality (that of a field antiquarian attached to the Rouen Faculty of Arts) that was to come.

He had merely been instructed to report for a special airborne course.

He had had no particular qualms about it, heights had never seriously bothered him, it was a change of camp, and any wold was better than the wold he was on at the moment. No, the whole thing had come as a complete shock to him.

He had arrived at the camp (near Cleethorpes) one Friday, and by Tuesday, after only vestigial training, he had been requested to climb into a basket attached to a very

74

large inflated silver condom accompanied by an Air Force Flight-Sergeant who regarded him with an expression of contemptuous commiseration.

Slowly the silver condom rose into the air, slowly the soggy green bosom of Lincolnshire was left behind, and slowly there dawned on him the enormity of what he had to do.

'This the first time you jumped, then, is it, sir?'

'Yes.'

'Shit-scared, most people are. Quite right too. If God had meant us to parachute he'd have given us telescopic kneecaps. Here we are, then. Let's be having you, sir.'

The Sergeant adjusted the harness while Tristram stole a glance over the side. This was a mistake. What he saw made him reel (difficult though such a movement was in a confined space) and claw instinctively at the Sergeant's uniform.

'I . . . can't . . . I won't . . .'

It was like being a child again. The years fell away, and at such a height, they went with a rush.

'Come along now, sir. I don't like to see an orficer clutch at my lapels. It lowers my opinion of the King's Commission.'

'But I'll fall.'

'That's the idea, sir. Though it might make a change if one of my gentlemen were to be borne aloft like Isaiah. Down seems such a one-way way, sir, if you see what I mean.'

'But it's ridiculous. No one in his right senses would just walk out of here.'

'Come along now, sir. Just stand on this little platform here by the gate, there you are, you're only 500 feet up, hardly enough to impact your legs in the event of misfortune, relax, bend your knees and roll over when you hit the ground. Easy as kiss my arse.'

Even in his panic, Tristram spared a moment for wonder

at the inappositeness of the phrase. (Embracing the Sergeant's sphincter would pose many problems.)

'No, no. I won't. I can't.'

Thank goodness Mother couldn't see him now. The Son of Cutcombe's heroic mould had suddenly gone soggy at the edges.

'D'you see that bushy-topped tree over there, sir?'

'What? Where? Over there?'

Tristram felt the Sergeant could have chosen a more tranquil moment to pursue his botanic enquiries.

'That's the one, sir? What sort of tree is that, sir?'

'I can't see. I think it's a . . . wooooooogh . . . '

Tristram felt a smart shove from behind, and suddenly he was outside the gondola. For an instant of unimaginable duration he seemed to hang above the airfield as though time, space and all the other forces of the Universe had suspended their laws in deference to the gravity (the pun only came to him later) of the situation.

And then down, down like glistering Phaethon, like a penny from Heaven or an egg off a tallboy, he dropped with a sensation in his stomach that could only have been invented in the new-product laboratories of the Goblin King working closely in association with Sawney Bean.

How he retained consciousness he never knew. He couldn't breathe. The wind bansheed in his ears, his arms and legs twirled endlessly in a grotesque parody of abandon, but the worst sensation of all was the sense of a total loss of personality, as though some succubus up in the aether was licking the very stuffing out of him, to leave him dangling and twirling for ever like a lost soul on God's clothes-peg.

Then suddenly the ground was coming towards him very fast, striking him a fearful buffet on the shoulder as he fell, and rolling him over and over amongst his rigging, in which he lay, trussed and twitching until the Sergeant came up wagging his head and asking him why he hadn't followed the correct procedure.

'You wait till you have to jump out of an aircraft at night in awkward terrain,' he said, reprovingly. 'Then you'll be sorry you didn't master directional control and touchdown drill like what Segeant Bickerstaff taught you. There you'll be, lying in the scrub, both legs broken, with Dobermann pinschers after you, and you'll think of me with tears, if I may say so, sir, of hopeless regret. Never mind that now, sir. You're wanted for survival training. Over to the Padre's office at the double if you would be so kind. You know what a stickler he is.'

And so it had gone on. Tristram had had two further jumps which caused him such acute terror that he toyed with the idea of going absent or shooting off his foot to avoid the final one they had scheduled for him — it was imperative for the Project, whatever the Project was, that he achieve a certain accuracy in his jump — but at the last moment he had been transferred to yet another camp for demolition training.

He knew, however, that he would have to jump again sooner or later, and the thought filled him, as the weeks passed and he became a walking compendium of martial information, from trembler fuses to cypher procedure, with a sense of impending and inescapable doom.

In other circumstances, had he been brought up differently and had a less robust terror of being found out, he might have told someone about his aversion, but he couldn't. The Son of Cutcombe could not be a coward. He could see his mother's expression as she learned of his failure. No, the thing had to be faced. The second time he went up not even the Sergeant could sense his abhorrence.

In peacetime it might have been called the beginning of a nervous breakdown. But a uniform does so much to hold a man together.

All this, tough though it was, might have been supported had there not been yet another consideration to ensnare his

77

rigging: Griselda. With some exercise of metathesis, their names, Tristram and Griselda, could be taken to form an approximation of the lovers of legend, so from the moment they met, there had been a certain whimsical bond, a bond which for his part rapidly grew into an all-embracing adhesion.

He had enjoyed her gentle romanticism, her sensitivity and lightness of touch, so different from the wilful egocentricity of his wife, so unlike the brutish and saturnine Franco. And yet, after all their meetings and conversations and one (admittedly unsatisfactory) night in London, she still would not leave Franco, there was still something there that held her and he thought he knew what it was. It wasn't romantic at all.

This, the fact that Griselda, while enjoying the nectars of romance, could still feed on earthier pleasures, caused him almost more pain than parachuting. And parachuting quite quickly started to give him a great deal of pain, because it was jumping from a moving aircraft now, which, though he had been informed to the contrary, was worse than leaping from a French letter.

And in the misty fastnesses of Wisbech and Boston, Lincs, with nothing else to think about, he developed an anguish that was almost Lear-like in its disillusion and self-disgust, all the worse because it was impossible to reveal.

And she, the only person he could be himself with, that sweet creature with the quick smile and the trout-pool eyes and the ready grasp of Beaumarchais' influence on the Revolution, how could she take down her knickers, open her legs and moan with delight at the crass thrustings of a dauber? 'From the waist down they are centaurs, though women all above.' What hell life was.

When he came down on leave a couple of times, it was better. It was bearable if he could see her. But, as the year progressed and he was posted further and further away, his anguish and passion became almost uncontainable.

It was at this stage that he had been sent for and told that the moment for which he had spent so many months preparing was at hand. The tortoise-headed Brigadier who spoke to him said that, for security reasons, they had decided against telling him what the mission was until the last moment, but they could now quite categorically assure him that he was to be dropped near Finisterre and proceed to a small farmhouse where he would rendezvous with a Resistance worker who would then accompany him to a certain wood near the coast. There he would collect certain information which he would then transmit by radio to England.

The tortoise-head said nothing about how he was to get back.

The culmination of so many months of strain, the terror of yet another jump over unknown and difficult terrain, the danger of the undertaking itself finally got through to him. He didn't crack. Outwardly he was perfectly controlled. His automatic pilot worked impeccably. But inside everything went curiously cloudy. His brain worked well, but he didn't seem to feel anything.

He remembered sitting in an Airedale-smelling staff car that conveyed them to an airfield. He dimly remembered taking off, flying uncomfortably for what seemed hours, and then, remarkably, jumping without the slightest sensation of fear. He had landed without harm, located the farmhouse, still with this strange sense of detachment, and he had been almost amused when he opened the door, expecting to be greeted by a genial if furtive Breton, and had found himself peering down the snout of a Schmeisser held by an SS officer.

As he turned the memory of the subsequent events over in his mind, he came once more to reflect on his present predicament. It was undeniably alarming, and yet somehow he could not make himself feel alarmed.

Before, he had merely felt detached, his mind simply shutting itself off from unpleasant experiences. But now, since the interview, he felt almost as if he had transferred into some kind of dream where he knew, if he really willed it, he would wake up. But, again, it wasn't quite like that, because he willed it, hard, and he didn't.

It was as if, in some strange way, he had switched from one track to another, but somewhere close at hand, the old track was running on beside him.

At this point in his meditation, the door opened and in walked the Gestapo officer again accompanied by an orderly carrying a tray containing a steaming mug. The officer motioned both the orderly and the guard outside, and placed the mug in front of Tristram.

'Now, Captain Sanderson, I hope you will have had time to reflect further on your ticklish situation here — and fortified by a cup of good old English tea, the cup that cheers but not inebriates, will soon find in yourself an overwhelming desire to speak with us. Proceed, Captain Sanderson. Sip. And then, as your American allies would say, sing. Like the linnet, Captain Sanderson, or indeed the darkling thrush. You have the beans. Let them now be spilled.'

But suddenly positive, though still dream-like, Tristram knew what to do. Instead of the beans, he spilled his mug of tea full in the Gestapo officer's face, causing him to lose his seemingly-inexorable control of the English language and his immaculately jack-booted balance.

'Aaaagh,' was all he could find to say as he floundered backwards, the cup that cheers searing his disdainful features as effectively, it seemed, as hydrochloric acid.

Tristram, seizing his moment and impelled by the automatic pilot that still seemed to be guiding his actions, sprang from his chair and flew head-first through the boarded window, picked himself up, shook off smashed wood like a dog, and becoming aware of a confused hubbub swelling behind him, scrambled over a low fence and raced for the cover of the trees.

He heard dogs baying, and an ominous pattern of earthcasts wriggled up beside him as a machine-gun opened fire from the camp.

With a last despairing lunge, he tumbled across another fence and threw himself into the bramble shadows.

13

There was thunder in that curious summer-thundery manner, both near and far away, almost it seemed on Cutcombe Hill and away far out over Dunkery. The sky, however, remained strangely clear.

The grownups had gathered in the drawing-room before dinner. It was going to be cream of watercress soup followed by gammon and peas and new potatoes, with rhubarb pie and Cutcombe cream to finish up with, and everyone was feeling rather good about it, including Franco and Griselda, who had been invited over at the last minute because old Mrs Sanderson was suffering from largesse-deficiency, and Thomas, who had been caught and pardoned by the Mother just as he was putting on his bicycle clips.

Upstairs, the boys were staring gloomily at the remains of their cereal and dried fruit, while Nanny prepared herself for the evening's pleasures in her boudoir next to the bathroom.

Rufus had put 'If I give up the saxophone, will you come back to me?' on the gramophone so that no one would hear him interrogating Adam over his conversation with the American.

'I hope you didn't mention anything. It would be viewed gravely. You don't know whether I've given you your dose tonight.'

'I didn't, honestly I didn't. But he kept asking questions.'

'What did he say?'

'Just things. He kept talking about birds. He asked me if I'd seen a monstrous owl.'

'And what did you say?'

'I told him I'd seen one.'

'Seen one? You never told me that. Why didn't you tell me that? You're supposed to keep me informed. Where did you see it?'

'It was in my mind. I saw it in my mind. I thought it was a Fright.'

'A Fright? You didn't tell him about the Frights?'

'No. No, I didn't. Honestly I didn't.'

Rufus had the knack of seeing everything in your mind, except, it seemed, monstrous owls.

'I'm glad to hear it, otherwise we might have to take certain steps. And another thing. I saw you taking him up the stream towards the Forbidden Zone. I hope you didn't tell him about the Forbidden Zone. The Frights would take a very dim view of that.'

'I didn't tell him about the Forbidden Zone. Honestly, Rufus.'

'That's all right, then.'

'Can I have my Sleeping Draught tonight?'

'Finish your Shredded Wheat. For all you know I may have given it to you already.'

Nanny appeared looking succulent in a light-green frock with her hair piled up high as one of Queenie's vol-au-vents (which you never got in the nursery), her cheeks blushing prettily and her eyes bright as marbles. She had managed to get a message to Rodgers, and he was staying late.

'Not finished yet? You're just pushing it around. Ought to be ashamed. Think of the starving children in China.'

They were welcome to his stale Shredded Wheat, and his gristly lumps of Irish stew and his fibrous vegetable marrow and his brawn with tubes and hair in and the awful frog-spawn blobs of tapioca. The starving children in China could have all the nursery food Cutcombe could send them until they cried for mercy and begged to be allowed to starve again. He had once suggested, over a particularly nauseating dish of matted swede, that he and Nanny put it in a parcel and despatch it simply to: Starving Children. China. But the idea had been rather firmly hit on the head, Nanny telling him he was a wicked little boy to make fun of other people's misfortunes.

Tonight, however, she seemed to be in better temper.

'Come along, slowcoach, Nanny can't go out until you're tucked up.'

Adam spooned manfully away, swallowed an apricot whole, and swooshed it down with milk like a ship going down the maelstrom.

'Finished, Nanny.'

His eyes were watering.

'Now both of you go and brush your teeth, and I want to hear you getting the potatoes out of your ears.'

'So we can send them to the starving children in China?'

But Nanny didn't think that was funny at all.

14

In the drawing-room, impatient to be at the nosebags, the company was listening to Granny Sanderson as she read aloud a letter from her son.

' "Lincolnshire has not yielded a fat crop of news these last few weeks. The weather has been undistinguished, the wolds have not show any tendency to skip like young sheep, and the Dutchmen are wearing flat. I went out shooting with a local farmer a couple of days ago and bagged some rabbits which we had cooked in genever gin — a mysterious taste . . . " '

Granny pronounced these offerings as though they were the Beatitudes.

'Not as toothsome as Cutcombe conies, I'll be bound.'

'Ugh. I don't know how he can eat rabbit. Like eating rat,' said Julia with a fastidious shiver, flashing a look of complicity at Thomas, who responded loyally if lyingly. He rather liked rabbit stew and had eaten it many times at summer camp, but what the hell, this was no moment for integrity.

Griselda sipped her drink and thought about the letter Tristram had sent her, poste restante at the Plume of Feathers in Dunster so no one would know.

'Darling Zelda,' it had read, 'I can't tell you how much I miss you. As much, in fact, as I hate this hellish life, so you see how extreme it is. The work is either boring or horrible, and the company . . . words fail me . . . like the Dutch. The nearest we get to conversation goes rather like this. "Pass the salt, please," "Pliss?" "The salt." "Der assault." "No." "Der assault on Nazis?" "No . . . don't bother." "Not bozzer mit assault on Nazis? Vot are you saying?" And so on. The awful thing is, the dreadful Dutch regard jumping as the greatest sport, and leap out of the plane as if they were tumbling into a sandpit, while all the time my knees are going like castanets. I have to keep my upper lip stiff to stop my heart flying out of my mouth. So many numbskulls can jump and yet it fills me with the utmost terror. What am I doing here? Why don't I tell them? Why am I surrounded by these incomprehensible

Dutch captains? No doubt I'll find out soon enough. I have the feeling it's all leading up to something big and dis-agreeable and rather imminent. If it is, I'd be glad in a way. I don't think I can go on like this much longer. Forgive me for whining on like this but there's no one else I can talk to . . . '

But his mother had finished her reading, and looked round triumphantly.

'There. You see? All that fuss about going to Lincolnshire as though it were the North Pole. Such nonsense. There are some wonderful houses up there. I told him to telephone the Le Blanc Smiths. He's having a whale of a time, silly old duffer, as well as doing work of the utmost importance, the utmost importance. He'll be a Major before we know where we are. So good for morale in the village. I'll just have another thimbleful if you press me, Chelly-Chops.'

'You and Franco have crossed each other's paths, I hear,' said Griselda to Thomas, who was staring at Julia as though she were about to pronounce an Ultimate Truth.

'Oh. Yes. We've met bicycling.'

On more than one occasion he had passed the Italian pedalling in the lanes, and once down by the sea sketching the distant hump of Watchet docks.

'Thomas is a great bicyclist,' said Julia, squeezing his arm secretly as if it were an inner tube.

'What else do you do? Before the war, I mean?' asked Granny Sanderson not very interestedly.

'Well, not all that much, actually. I er . . . '

'But is a great bicyclist,' smiled Franco, sporting amongst the conversation like a sardonic pilchard. 'A man does not have to be more.'

'Certainly,' said Julia. 'Why should he? It's better than trying to be a great artist, for instance. It's better to lift a balloon gracefully than to make a fool of yourself with the dumb-bells.'

85

Thomas flushed a look of gratitude at her as Franco seemed momentarily discomfited. At the same time, he couldn't help feeling puzzled. There was something about the room, the whole conversation, her sudden interpolation of a brilliant remark, that struck him as being positively other-worldly, quite unlike the one he was used to in which hardly anything seemed to go his way.

Chelly-Chops watched them with secret malevolence while she poured Granny Sanderson a measure of Gordons as meticulously as if it had been prussic acid, pausing only to tweak her hearing aid to max so as not to miss the slightest nuance of mischief.

She could tell them all a thing or two, but she wasn't going to. Not yet. She would shoot her mouth off (she had a weakness for American gangster films) only when she was good and ready, and then let them cringe and lick her dubbin by the mouthful.

15

Griselda and Tristram had spent a night together in London. It was this that had convinced her that Tristram, though incredibly handsome in a young-Apollo-golden-haired kind of way, and a sensitive and amusing companion at times, perhaps a little too sensitive when you got to know him (which nobody but she apparently did), could never take the place of Franco in bed.

It was shocking to her to admit, at last, that this side of things mattered, and worse that it seemed to matter more than everything else. Bad luck, of course, for Tristram that

Franco was so good — it made his shortcomings all the more glaring.

Tristram had had a forty-eight-hour leave. It coincided with a phase in which she was growing more and more irritated with Franco's mocking egocentricity. And she finally agreed, after urgent communication, to meet the Son of Cutcombe in a small hotel near South Kensington station. She told Franco that she had to go to Town to see her mother who was in for an operation, and after an exhausting jouney of nearly eight hours (a bomb on the line near Reading) she arrived in the modest establishment and had to wait in a freezing bedroom for another three before he finally turned up (delayed by troop movements in Chelmsford).

She wasn't in the least bit cross really, just bored and cold and rather tired, but it had somehow taken the edge off the situation. They had gone to a show but the show was indifferent. They had ordered champagne for supper but it seemed curiously flat. Nothing seemed to work. There weren't any taxis around to take them back. But it was when they reached their bedroom that the real trouble started.

She had gone to the bathroom to undress and slip into her pretty peach coloured nightdress, and when she came back she rather hoped he would be decently between the sheets with his head poking out like a pixie.

Instead, he was pacing about the room, fully-dressed, and smoking. She hated smoking in the bedroom.

'Come to bed, darling.'

The endearment sat as strangely on her lips as Cutcombe quince jelly.

Tristram shook his head and continued pacing.

'I don't think I can carry on like this much longer,' he said.

Griselda suppressed a sigh. It wasn't exactly the romantic outcome she had envisaged. The gallant hero seemed to be falling short on both heroism and gallantry, and she looked so nice in her peach nightdress. She felt sympathy for him, of course she did, but she hadn't spent eight hours in the train for sympathy.

When, finally, she had coaxed him into bed, her expectations were still further diminished by the tidy way he folded his uniform. It smacked of pedantry rather than passion. Still, she had turned over and kissed him tenderly, but even then he had not taken her in his arms with the ebullience of Franco and done shameful wonderful things with his hands, but had made one or two diffident moth-like sweeps and then, at the crucial moment, failed to achieve an erection. She wouldn't have minded, really she wouldn't, but it seemed to affect him dreadfully.

'I can't even get that right,' he kept saying. 'Even the cowman can do it and I can't. It's like the bloody jumping. Everyone except me.'

'Perhaps we need some sort of aphrodisiac,' she suggested desperately, not quite knowing where to lay hands on one.

'There's only one aphrodisiac that'd do me any good,' he replied moodily. 'A snake-charmer in the bedroom.'

She had tried to comfort him but he seemed inconsolable.

It had not been a satisfactory weekend.

16

The gong in the hall had sounded for dinner a good half-hour ago and Adam was lying in bed, sprawled across the cool sheets, like a runner pressed in glass, waiting to go to sleep. He knew he would very soon because of the Sleeping Draught, but he was disturbed in his drowsiness by Rufus.

'Come on.'

'Come on what?'

'Come and get up. We've got to go and see where Nanny's gone!'

Adam was shocked. The danger was appalling.

'We can't.'

'We jolly well can. Don't be a funk. Cowardy custard.'

'What about the Frights? What if they come and they find us?'

'They don't come till much later.'

'What about the Sleeping Draught? I might suddenly fall asleep.'

Adam pictured himself log-like on the drive.

'I gave you a delayed-action one.'

'But . . . we don't know where she's gone.'

'Down to the barn. She's with Rodgers.'

'With Rodgers? What . . . what do they do there?'

'They have a drink and they . . . '

'They what?'

'You'll see.'

'I . . . I don't want to.'

'You know what happens when you fail to obey orders.'

'I've had my Sleeping Draught tonight.'

'It won't help you tomorrow.'

It was all very well for Rufus, but he knew who'd be the one to get caught. And anyway he wasn't particularly interested in where Nanny was and what Nanny was doing. He saw quite enough of Nanny by day, thank you very much.

'Field Marshal Ball is waiting, Adam. I hope we're not going to have to have a Court-Martial.'

Adam started to struggle into his Aertex shirt.

17

Chelly-Chops gazed across the impressive Podsnappery of silver cellars and candelabra, across the great gleaming brown Limpopo of the table, to where Granny Sanderson sat at the end wreaking terrible havoc on a roll and curly Cutcombe butter while they waited for the soup.

How had she got into this, trapped for ever with these people? She almost prayed for the Germans to come because it would do so much to shake their complacency.

'The Headmaster always told me Tristram would do well in the wider seas of life,' said the Granny, chasing a ball of butter round the bowl.

How Chelly-Chops hated those phrases. The wider seas of life indeed. She had never found the seas of life wider. In fact, the further she went on, the narrower and more straitened they became.

'The dried-up creek of life, more like,' she mumbled as Queenie from the kitchen brought in a brimming tureen.

'What's that, Chell?' demanded the Granny suspiciously, her ears as alert as sonar scanners. 'Mumbling again? Turn up your twangling instrument. Can't hear yourself speak, that's your trouble. Won't be able to hear yourself think, next.'

It wasn't her fault she was deaf. She had started all right, a country vicar's daughter, nicely brought up, plain but unexceptionable, a modestly good education, the very stuff of minor county wifehood, and then one day someone had prankishly pushed her while playing near the school swimming-pool, she never knew who but she wished them perdition, and she had fallen in, striking her head viciously on the concrete edge.

She had nearly drowned, and there were times when she wished that she had, although her kindly parents had done everything a slender income would allow to make up to her for her misfortune. Because, from that moment, without a powerful hearing aid that seemed to weigh half a ton, even the canons bawling across the transept in the local cathedral sounded like pixies calling shyly in a fog. She was almost completely deaf.

To add to her misfortunes, both her parents had been killed in a motoring accident while touring remote churches in the Bas Pyrenees, though why they should go to such lengths in pursuit of mouldy old churches she could never understand, and now never would. And after sundry unpleasant and chastening experiences being locked in her own silent head in the midst of inimical strangers, she finally had no recourse, being untrained and without funds, but to let herself be taken in by some cousins of her mother's who lived in deepest Somerset.

That had all been years back, but she was still here. She would be here for life: handmaiden, buffoon and bond-slave to the tyrannical old spider who now sat before her shovelling down croutons. While she, Antoinette Chelford, spinster of this parish, could have been as much a success as any of them, including that pirouetting daughter-in-law who certainly did not deserve the hand of the Son of Cutcombe, even though he wasn't all he was cracked up to be — and she could tell a thing or two about his carryings-on with that pi-faced artist-wife, butter wouldn't melt in her mouth, even the curly Cutcombe kind, but she shouldn't leave letters lying around, should she? As for the fawning devotion of that bookish Yank, every time he looked at the daughter-in-law, it made her want to gag on her potage du jour. A long time ago, a young Lieutenant, barely nineteen had looked at her like that. He didn't know she was deaf of course, at least she never heard whether he did or not but he never came back from Passchendaele otherwise he

91

might have climbed up her plaits and set her free.

So here she was, imprisoned at Cutcombe, and locked quietly inside herself with her own unwelcome thoughts. Really, she thought, a warder should come in every day and remove them. No, not so much a gaol, she corrected herself, more like a padded cell, noiseless, except when she had the uncertain help of her lump of a hearing aid, and even that transmitted some most peculiar effects which she could never tell were in her head or the machine or indeed the very ether. There was sometimes for instance, late at night, the most peculiar morse-like noise, as though someone were transmitting, but that didn't seem very likely, not round Cutcombe way. Trust the old spider to call it a twangling instrument. It was easy to mock.

She looked about her again. What were they all saying? Suddenly she wanted to talk to them, to make them understand.

'Life is like a funnel,' she wanted to tell them, 'wide at the top but getting narrower as you go down.'

But she knew they would secretly either laugh, because she spoke too loudly, or simply bend a sarcasm in her direction – a revenue she normally returned with interest, but somehow she didn't feel like it just now.

So all she said was, 'Pass the pepper, please,' in a hoarse little voice that nobody seemed to hear.

She sighed. There was too much salt in the soup again.

Thomas, sitting next to Chelly-Chops, was placed opposite Julia and he was in buoyant mood. Nothing could depress him – old Mrs Sanderson's overweening complacency, Chell's adder-like asides – life at every turn was coming up with roses.

Her hair was shiningly chestnut, her skin so mouth-wateringly fresh, and though she was neither intellectual nor erudite, she had a kind of delicate vibrancy about her which made you feel that to be near her was to be alive and to be absent was the dark side of the moon.

As she tucked into her Cutcombe gammon and garden peas, it was impossible to imagine that they would be converted by her digestive processes into a medley of fats, amino acids, sugar and wastes, but they would instead convert into gold and gossamer influences leaving not so much as a thistledown of detritus. She did not have the normal grosser functions, but merely wept like a flower. If he could bite her delicately curved mouth, he would not ask for rashers.

These considerations passed through his mind as the conversation ranged from the state of the kitchen garden to the conduct of the war. Desperately wishing to impress her, he cast about for an opportunity.

Across the table, Franco was talking to the Grandmother about concentration camps and God. Old Mrs Sanderson prided herself on her special relationship with the Almighty, and had made it quite clear on a previous occasion that if He were to consider sending his Son to take on the mantle of flesh at any future juncture, she personally would view his career with considerable interest and quite possibly ask him over to dinner.

On this occasion, however, she professed herself foxed.

'How can God allow such terrible things to happen?' she said, mopping up some gravy with a gobbet of baked potato, and indicating that if the Divine Will did not mend its ways she might have to review her subscription for the church roof fund.

Franco cocked his head on one side and looked duly concerned.

'And how can your countrymen,' she continued, never scorning to hit a man when he was down, 'how can your countrymen, like Michelangelo and Plutarch or do I mean Petrarch, who've created such frightfully beautiful things in the name of God, how can they ally themselves with an Anti-Christ like like Hitler?'

Franco steered a piece of gammon round and round his

plate, peas bubbling in its wake like acoustic mines. He appeared to be giving the overworked subject the utmost attention, as if she had queried the ontology of Heidegger.

'A good question, Mrs Sanderson,' he adjured at length, 'is a very good question. This is what I ask myself. I am ashamed of my countrymen's fall from grace. This is why I not return to the land of my birth. You have expression: the higher they rise, the harder they fall. That is what has happened to Italy. A lesson for mankind, Mrs Sanderson, I assure you. Very good gravy indeed.'

The Granny took the change of subject effortlessly. She was always prepared to expatiate on the subject of Cutcombe excellence and frankly felt the Italians could stew in their own juice.

'Cutcombe gravy has always been admired. A secret I passed on to Queenie. These people never baste enough.'

'Why not you make gravy like this, Zelda? The English passion for gravy has always induced in me a lively dolour, Mrs Sanderson, until I come to your hospitable board.'

The Grandmother simpered. She was highly susceptible to sycophancy and Franco was, when it suited him, a master of the art. Tonight, he had cast himself in the role of her jester.

'Grave. Gravy. Gravity. What a lot of different meanings the English extract from their syllables. Is like the Italian way with pigs. Use everything except the bones.'

'Ha. Ha. Ha.'

The Grandmother was so amused her plaits nearly uncoiled.

Griselda, however, was embarrassed. It was partly the piercing little looks Chell kept shooting at her (what had happened to that letter?), but mostly that she hated to see Franco making fun of people, even when the victim was so richly deserving. She felt sure the Grandmother must realize she was being mocked.

'Ha ha ha,' the Grany was drawing every ounce of mirth

and more from the Italian's jape, shaking like a junket in her dark-brown dress and drawing an appalled glance from Chelly-Chops.

'Sausages of sound, Mrs Sanderson. Salamis of sense.'

Even Julia started laughing.

Thomas felt he was losing ground, and cast about earnestly for wit or wisdom, but once more Franco was there before him.

'Spinoza says,' Thomas's heart sank as it always did at the mention of the thin spidery name, 'Spinoza tell us that we must not look for a narrow interpretation, we must not how you say examine the trees, we must concentrate on the wood.'

Thomas wanted to say he doubted if Spinoza ever had his little daughter torn from his arms, raped and then beaten to a pulp with the butt of a rifle, but he felt this might cast too much of a chill on the proceedings.

'You mean . . . ' you could see the bobbins of the Grandmother's mind whirling and agitating like Arkwright's Mule, 'you mean, God works in a mysterious way his wonders to perform?'

'You are very educated woman, Mrs Sanderson, very sensitive. Exactly. It is not easy for us to believe in the infinite goodness of the Almighty when we have a teethache or a pain in the stomacco, but it is all part of a plan that leads us to Perfection.'

Franco shovelled in more peas, nodding his head emphatically so that they shot about the aperture of his mouth like magma in Stromboli.

Thomas, who had recently been reading a Life of Darwin as part of his policy of metaphysical self-improvement, suddenly saw his chance.

'Which leads one on,' he said quickly, blinking a bit, 'to postulate . . . '

'Don't look, ladies,' cried Franco merrily, 'is not nice to postulate at table.'

95

'Idiot,' said Griselda, laughing immoderately in spite of herself.

The Grandmother paused for a moment, fork to mouth, staring from one to another with the beadiness of an old guinea-fowl, uncertain whether to exercise her prerogative and rule that her pet artist had gone too far, but eventually gave him the benefit of the doubt and joined in the general mirth at Thomas's expense.

He looked about him, appalled at their careless malice, not daring to see how Julia was taking it. Only Adam and Rufus, sitting over the sideboard in Franco's portrait, appeared to be taking a detached and intelligent interest, and now he looked harder even Rufus seemed to be wearing the ghost of a sneer.

'What did he say?' croaked Chell, twiddling her twangler.

Thomas, blushing furiously decided there was only one way to go.

'Which leads one to postulate,' he repeated as the room once more rocked to the familar Cutcombe din of people laughing at other people's expense, 'that there may perhaps be a Darwinian interpretation of Evil. Just as in the Cell and indeed the Species there is a constant tension between Perfect Reproduction,' he sensed a snigger from Franco's direction, 'and Mutation, resulting in an ever-improving Evolution, so the struggle between Good and Bad leads to an ever-improving quality of Spirit. Good is simply the straight cell, Evil the mutation. Neither must be confused with the end-product. The only problem is, where does Original Sin fit in? You can't blame the first cell that went wrong for the seed of change implanted in it any more than you can blame humanity. In the beginning was the Word and the Word was God and the Word was with God but one of its serifs was broken. Why should we have to go through this Officer Selection course on the way to Life Immortal?'

Thomas had never stuck his head out so far across the lengthy chopping-block of Cutcombe society, and sat back with a mixture of elation and diffidence, diffidence rapidly gaining the upper hand.

'Sorry to go on like that,' he said, waving his hands disassociatingly, 'just been reading the Voyage of the Beagle. You know how it is.'

Griselda had stopped laughing and now gave him something like a sympathetic but it could have been pitying smile. The Grandmother, however, frowned. It was clear that he had in some way committed a gaffe, but she found herself once again undecided which offence to punish him for: was it a case of straightforward blasphemy or was the young man too clever by half, the most heinous crime in the Cutcombe canon?

She pursed her lips, from which an audacious frond of vegetable still waved, relishing her decision.

The Italian busied himself with his wineglass, making little swilling noises as the claret sloshed through his incisors.

Chelly-Chops hadn't heard most of it anyway so it didn't matter.

It was Julia's verdict that mattered. For an awesome second, her expression remained ambiguous.

At this juncture, the progress of Cutcombe dinner was interrupted by a totally unforeseen and indeed unforeseeable development.

For some time, it was true, Thomas had felt a certain electricity in the air, but whether it was induced by the normal Cutcombe atmosphere of comfort-with-danger which was Old Mrs Sanderson's particular stock in trade, intimations of immorality with Julia, or simply the leaden aspect of the evening sky, shot through with flickerings of summer lightning and punctuated by rumblings from above as if a very old man were moving statues in the attic, he could not accurately assess.

Whatever his source of anticipation, he suddenly became aware of a bluish light suffusing the room which seemed to be coming from the fireplace, and which, as he looked round, provided a spectacular effect of halation round each person sitting at the table.

Before he had time to articulate his astonishment with so much as a gurgle, a bluish orangey ball of contained flame like a faulty street lamp crashed down the chimney and rolled out into the room with a slow but as it were informed deliberation. At which point, it paused.

Thomas experienced the most extraordinary sensations while this was taking place, but was unable now to compare notes with his dining companions since everyone present, even the informed fireball, seemed to be locked in a strange rictus, and he himself felt like one of those products in Perspex which his father used to receive from industrial clients for Christmas. Perhaps this was death, he reflected, people had got it wrong, you just stayed like that, frozen but aware until you went mad.

However, at this point the ball started to move again — moving, astonishingly, alarmingly, towards himself (why me?), and finally enveloping him in a radiance that seemed to pierce the very centre of his being. He felt as though his entire body, the room, the house, the past, the present and whatever future there might be were being intolerably stretched, dislocated and spun again like a Chinaman making noodles.

Even while all this was happening, part of him was watching with physicist's eyes, and there was something half-remembered, something he had read, that gave the whole remarkable display a quite momentous significance. It was Gödel, he felt sure, who'd written it, something about the phenomenon of globe lightning, and the eccentricity of particle-waves under certain electrical conditions. If Time was indeed splitting with every microsecond that passed, it might be that in the vicinity of globe lightning it was possible for a trained observer to note some iota of variation . . . it was Gödel, wasn't it . . .

He supposed he must momentarily have passed out, for when he looked around him again, everything was as it had been before the interruption. Indeed, perhaps the most extraordinary thing of all was that nobody appeared to have noticed it. They were all eating or swigging as if nothing more remarkable than a hawkmoth had dropped in.

Thomas, though amazed, put it down to English sang-froid, and deemed that it might be considered loutish to comment on anything, whatever the circumstances, ill-mannered enough to disturb a Cutcombe dinner. But just at this point, Julia gave him something else to think about as she leant across under the table and squeezed his knee. Trained physicist or no, his cosmic speculations were considerably deranged by the slight, warm, silky pressure, and he reverted to earlier intimations. His instinct in the drawing-room had not been wrong. Come when it would, if he wasn't very much mistaken, the Problem of Evil was soon going to be more than a purely academic affair.

'We had a beagle once,' announced Chell, crushingly, 'but we certainly never found him a problem apart from his ear.'

Thomas experienced a darting sensation that everything was not quite as it seemed, that if he could lift a flap he would see the whole dinner party going on with a completely different tone imprinted on it, but with Chell one often experienced a sense of dislocation.

Had he imagined the whole affair, was it some kind of momentary quirk of digestion, a split-second brainstorm induced by love and St Emilion, or had he really experienced the thing that he had so often dreamed of, a manifestation of the duality of Time itself?

Whatever it was, he needed time to think about it, but at the moment (it was Julia's foot nudging him this time) there were more pressing matters in hand.

'I daresay,' concluded Chell, with a look of loathing that would have done credit to a boletus satanicus, 'not being English, you didn't look after yours properly.'

Thomas noticed that Franco seemed to be having trouble keeping his peas in his mouth.

18

The night was rather like the inside of Jackie Jewel's potting shed, dusky and still and shot through with a cowy, middeny, vegetably sort of smell. There were lumpy things too which didn't seem to be there by day.

Adam clutched hold of Rufus, who scuttled purposefully across the drive and down the shrubbery steps to the stables.

'What if they find us?' he said.

Rufus did not reply but pressed on even faster, his gym shoes making a squeaky noise on the slate.

'I'm sleepy,' Adam said, 'are you sure the Sleeping Draught's not working?'

'Of course it isn't. I calculated your dose for a Night Operation.'

'What if the Frights come early? There's lumpy things over there.'

Rufus stopped abruptly and peered into the gloom.

'That's a rhododendron, stupid. Anyway, the Frights never come early. They have no power to. Come on. We've got to observe silence from now on. This is the tricky bit.'

They crept across the cobbled yard in the direction of the

cowman's cubbyhole. There was a thin trickle of light coming from a chink in the blanketed window. Rodgers must have got his oil-lamp on, but turned down very low. Cautiously, they inched forward, Adam marking Rufus's footsteps in case of crackly things on the ground, like the page in Good King Wenceslas.

When they reached the shelter of the wall, Rufus stopped, motioning Adam back with army hand signs. In the glow from the window, Adam could see him steal forward, crouch under the sill, and then gently raise his head over the lip. He stood there immobile for what seemed like the duration of one of the Reverend Biddle's geological ages (he came over, in term time, twice a week to teach them the rudiments). The Cambrian was well spent and Adam was trying to remember what came after it, when Rufus made a sound, a sort of cross between a whistle and a gasp of excitement.

'What is it? What's happening?'

'Shhhhhhhh.'

Finally Adam could bear it no longer, and tiptoed up to the window himself, gingerly raising his head to peer at whatever it was that held his brother so engrossed.

His cautious gaze took in a scene that, though unprecedented and in many ways puzzling, had an absolutely forbidden quality about it, a No-Children-Here-ness like the library after lunch, or Chelly-Chops scanning the corridor before she went into the lav. It was like that, but very very much worse.

Nanny lay on her back, her mouth open with a look of almost painful concentration on her face, her frock undone to the waist with her breasts flopping out, a big red button on each like a glacé cherry and her skirt up to her thighs hardly covering the rude bits which appeared to be resting on Rodgers's face.

The really shocking part about it was that somehow he had expected grownups to be different, undressed, and here they were looking just like children, give or take a little hairiness.

At this point, straining almost against his will to get a better view, he trod on an old piece of kindling wood propped between the ground and the wall.

It snapped with a report like a twelve-bore, throwing the occupants of the cubbyhole into a frenzy of activity. Out popped Rodgers's shiny face, in popped Nanny's unbridled bosom, and off scooted the boys into the shelter of the stable wall.

'Stupid idiot,' hissed Rufus, 'now you've gone and done it. It was just getting to the interesting bit. Trust you to mess it up.'

'It wasn't my fault,' said Adam, 'and anyway I didn't like it. I wish I hadn't come.'

'Come on out,' shouted Rodgers, now trousered, swinging a lantern from the doorway.

'Doo'ee come back in,' said Nanny, ''twas only an old cat or summat.'

'Don't be so sure,' said Rodgers, stepping for a hideous second towards their wall, and then at the last minute changing his mind.

'Can we go to bed now? I'm sleepy,' said Adam, as the cubbyhole banged shut again.

'Sleepy? You're a fine one for a night patrol. They didn't scale the Heights of Abraham whining about sleep to General Wolfe. "Please, General, can we do it in the morning,' 'cos we're soooo tired?" ' said Rufus, leading the way up the steps again towards the pale cloudiness of the house. He seemed to be not at all astounded by the revelations of the evening. Did he go down there every night?

As for himself, he thought he'd never be able to look Nanny in the face again. He'd always be thinking of her Forbidden Zone, the one she had been showing to Rodgers. The other thing was, he still couldn't get over how

102

like children they had seemed.

Perhaps that's why grownups are so keen to keep children at a distance, he thought. We're much too like them for comfort.

19

'Here is the nine o'clock news and this is Alvar Liddell reading it . . . There has been a major offensive by the Axis in the foothills of the . . . '

The Grandmother sat at her dressing-table, reflecting on the night's news, with her long hair, normally strictly plaited and coiled, now unleashed and running wild about her face, a travesty of the burnished waterfall that had so delighted her late husband Frederick.

'Sport'st in the gilt plaits of thy beams,' Old Frederick would say, a long time ago when he had been the Young Lochinvar and she had been the child-bride, carried away from her triumphant debut on the London stage (had she not got 'See you at rehearsal, J.M. Barrie' in her commonplace book?) to this remote castle in the combes, where she had devoted all her talent, energy and dedication to making the production a success.

A success it had undoubtedly been. Was she not a JP at the local magistrates' court? Had not Cutcombe Women's Institute romped home with the Somerset Drama Prize for three years in a row? What more did she have to do? And yet, the thought would sneak into her mind, what had she gained by it?'

'On the home front, Fighter Command repulsed a raid

against Southampton early this morning with heavy enemy losses . . . '

She was in low spirits tonight. The thing was, which she hadn't told anyone, she was half-Jewish. Her mother, whom she had always kept, till her death, in the background in Kent, had had the maiden name of Lewis — but it was really Levi. And ever since before the war even started, Granny had been obsessed with the thought that one day the Nazis would arrive, strip her of her office and make her sweep the roads quite possibly all the way to Dunster.

It was the only thing in that long and tiresome life ('Mrs Sanderson? A fine woman. There's no trouble she won't put you to.') which had ever managed to shake her.

She had survived childbirth with flying colours, the doctor and nurses falling readily into the proper postures of adulation as she lay on her back and waited for the juvenile lead to make his appearance.

'Really, Mrs Sanderson, you're the pefect patient.'

True she had moaned a little once or twice when it was going on, but it had been so prettily done, so well modulated, which wasn't surprising because, though the doctor and nurse didn't know it, she had rehearsed the part five years previously when she had played the child-wife in the Tree production of David Copperfield.

'It didn't hurt at all,' she said later, lightly, 'just rather an effort, like walking up Cutcombe Hill in wet weather,' though it was noted that she didn't essay the experience a second time.

She had survived Tristram's going to school, crying prettily into her handkerchief as she put him on the train.

She had survived her father's death (her mother's was allowed to pass largely unnoticed). She looked good in black and enjoyed the grandiloquence of the service.

' "He fleeth as it were a shadow and never continueth in one stay" . . . So austere but so rich,' she would say at a seemly distance afterwards, 'so toothsome. You can taste the syllables like bitter Suchard.'

She had survived the discovery of her husband's minor peccadilloes with funny people like tobacconist's assistants in Minehead, simply by appearing to ignore them.

And, six years ago, she had survived his demise.

Though initially exuberant, tasteful and charming, he had become towards the end an increasingly shadowy figure, his traits eroded by the reiterated tide of her personality. Like Delilah, she had been captivated by his strengths, and like Delilah she had ended up curtailing them.

She had survived the advent of old age. But the Germans were different. It was, of course, out of the question that Churchill would allow them to arrive, but there was a nasty little inkling at the back of her mind that one day the knock at the door would come and it would be them with a Star of David specially for her.

And, after the mandatory torments of interrogation, her new star role would be to work in the fields with Rodgers, or be made into a lampshade.

She touched the puffy skin of her cheek. 'Let your light so shine before men.'

'Jüdin. Jüdin.'

And what of Tristram? What if he were captured and his Jewish connection discovered?

She knew she ought to tell him. But how could she admit such an imperfection?

'A Jew, Mother?'

She hoped she wasn't going to have those curiously lifelike and quite insupportable dreams again. She touched her cheek once more. Everything seemed strangely unrooted as though she were floating somewhere between her reflection and her face. 'And like this insubstantial pageant faded, leave not a wrack behind.' Perhaps one would simply vanish like the Baker in the Snark.

She shivered. Where was Chelly-Chops with her hot milk?

20

Thomas bicycled down the pitted drive in the breathing darkness with his eyes shining like headlamps and his heart held high.

All Julia's tender side had suddenly been granted to him. The petulance had vanished, she had smiled secretly not once but many times, and the memory of their walk after dinner on the verandah among the trays of bonsai trees rode sweetly with him under the pleaching oak trees.

She had kissed him almost at once, as soon as they had left the drawing-room where Chelly-Chops for all her deafness was playing Haydn (execrably) on the rosewood spinet.

'The Germans are supposed to like music, aren't they?' he said, balancing the coffee cups. 'We ought to aim her at them as our secret weapon.'

And suddenly the perfect mouth was on his, plump and firm as a lychee and tasting of wine and raspberries.

'Darling, darling,' he gasped, sloshing the coffee dangerously across the saucers, and cramming them down in double quick time on top of a bonsai basin, a violation from which at least one dwarf fir never fully recovered.

'Darling,' he repeated, not exactly originally, he felt, always the self-critic, but nothing else quite seemed to fill the bill.

He could feel her body, lithe and slippery as a Cutcombe trout, under the delicious sleekness of her dress.

Inside, the spinet tinkled on indefatigably (Chelly-Chops deaf to all entreaties). Outside, the night boiled with a billion stars. Thomas felt universal stirrings within him.

All the doubts and pains of the past seemed to be assuaged.

'Darling,' he said again, louder this time.

'Shhh. You'll drown the poor Broadwood.'

'I'd like to. Or turn it into a string orchestra.'

They struggled fervently together in the rose-scented darkness. The very night seemed to possess and envelop them, irresistibly forcing them deeper and deeper into the creamy darkness at the centre of a vast Morning Glory.

'Please,' he said, sensing his powerlessness to alter the outcome but nonetheless clutching at her bosoms like a drowning man, 'please can we, please.'

'Not now,' she said, pushing him gently away, very gently away, 'greedy pig.'

'But when? Where?'

'All things come to him who waits.'

'But when?'

She disengaged herself, putting a hand to his lips. Once again, he was aware of a curiously dreamlike sensation, that the sequence of events had long ago been decided and that all power of decision and action had been taken from him.

'Come over on Saturday,' she said, 'before the party. In the afternoon. We'll have a picnic tea up on the Quarry.'

'Just you and me?'

'Just you and me and the fritillaries.'

So odd, he reflected as he sped down the last few yards of the drive, so odd of her to be using such phrases, to have been keeping them concealed for so long, the wit and the sensitivity he had been so much wanting to hear from her.

As he shot out from the tunnel of trees into Cutcombe Lane, the sky was suddenly revealed between the high beech walls, shining like a celestial canal and speckled with a dogfish's dinner of starry plankton.

He realized that his imagination, fired by the evening's events, was working overtime, but he could have sworn he had seen, in the phosphorescence, just where the drive

107

turned into the road, a dim but familiar figure sidling behind a tree.

On reflection, it seemed most improbable that the Italian or indeed anyone but the Beast of Brendon would be wandering around at this hour, so he dismissed the notion as a trick of the shadows.

He had better things to think about.

21

Adam was having a nightmare.

Though he knew he was asleep, he was somehow able to see into a bedroom, which, dully revealed by fitful moonlight, he recognized as his own.

He knew that he must be sleeping in Rufus's old bed, however, because the figure in the other bed certainly wasn't him, nor, he was certain, was it Rufus. He didn't have an uninterrupted field of vision, though, because the old screen with all the pictures and cut-outs pasted on it had been placed near where he lay, only allowing him a narrow view of the doorway and the other bedhead.

He knew that something terrible was going to happen, and he tried to concentrate on the familiar jolly cut-outs, but somehow they only made it worse.

'Johnny and Rover and Susan and I
Went out to the fields to play.'

The children weren't smiling at him though, they were sneering, and the jolly dog slavered. Then, to his horror, the door started to open, the handle turning with infinite slowness. He wanted to scream, hide under the bedclothes, anything, but he was gripped by a terrible powerlessness, so that he could only watch.

As the door slowly creaked open, a long reptilian snout appeared round the corner, wagging a little this way and that to see how the land lay.

Satisfied, it moved forward revealing a scaly body, man-shaped, apart from its hideous head and tail and claws. It walked, though quietly, with a sort of horrible confidence, as if it were perfectly familiar with its territory and was only anxious that it should not be betrayed before it was absolutely ready.

Adam started moaning in his sleep.

'No . . . no . . . take them away . . . '

The creature turned towards the door, evil finger to lip, and made a beckoning motion. Immediately more figures, spawn of some grotesque vision of medieval hell, started to flow in from the darkness outside. There was a figure with a fish's head, another like a toad, a pale worm with burning eyes, and a Looking-Glass man with a huge head and a tiny body.

As they entered, they made almost no noise, but Adam could just hear the scrape of claws and the soft suck of wet pads on the linoleum.

They gathered about the bed, but just a little distance away from it so as not to disturb the sleeper, who now began to move fretfully under the pink eiderdown with goldilock bears on it. They seemed to be waiting for something.

'Don't let him wake up,' Adam moaned.

Terrified though he was, he tried desperately hard to warn the occupant of the bed to stay asleep.

The feathers started to blow in through the doorway. Even the gloating figures round the bed stopped their horrible leering and craning, as though at the approach of something momentous, drawing back a little more.

A vast white shadow seemed to be gathering in the

passage beyond the door. Slowly, with hideous deliberation, it grew, and slowly it advanced, its shape, whatever it
was, obscured by the swirling blizzard of feathers around
it.

'The Owl. The Monstrous Owl.'

Now it had come, Adam knew that he had been expecting it.

The other creatures cowered and fell back still further as
the huge shape, half man, half bird, approached the bed
and loomed over the sleeper.

'Don't wake up,' Adam screamed.

But it was no good. Just at that moment, the recumbent
figure, it was a fully-grown man, opened his eyes and sat
bolt upright with a cry of fear and disgust. And, as if at a
signal, upon the sound, the entire freakish company fell
upon him and though he struggled convulsively, bore him
screaming from the room.

Just as they were leaving, the very last to go, a sort of sly
conspiratorial larky-looking creature, put its head on one
side and looked straight at Adam, shocking him because
somehow he had felt they hadn't known he was there, that
he was just a spectator.

'You next,' the creature said, 'you next. Any more for
the Skylark?'

'Shut up,' said Rufus, 'you'll wake the whole house.'

Adam looked up and saw his brother's serious little face
gazing down at him. Already the darkness was drawing up
its skirts, like old Mrs Allacott paddling at Blue Anchor,
showing the first bashful intimations of grey. Suddenly
everything seemed very safe and very normal.

'It was the Frights,' he said, 'I saw the Frights.'

Rufus, contrary to Adam's expectations, did not seem
impressed. In fact, he appeared quite vexed with the
information.

'Liar,' he said, 'you couldn't possibly've. The Frights
didn't come last night. No one did. I know because I put a

hair across the door and it was still there when I came in.'

He padded across, bent down by the key hole, and brought something over. Sure enough, there was a hair dangling from a blob of green Plasticine. Plasticine smelt funny in the almost dark, out of place, Adam decided, belonging to daytime, like the smell of Turkish cigarettes in the hall after breakfast, or kedgeree. He peered at it uncertainly.

'See,' said Rufus, 'they couldn't have come.'

'But I saw them,' said Adam, obstinately. 'I saw the Monstrous Owl.' But the memory was fading even as he spoke.

Did Rufus always put hair across the door? Why had he not mentioned it before? The trouble was, you could never tell with Rufus, it might be just a military precaution to see the room wasn't booby-trapped, or that they weren't spied on by Nanny. Or it might be that he was just as scared of the Frights as Adam was, but he didn't think for a moment that could be the case because Rufus had always given the impression he had a sort of Red Cross immunity as far as the terrors that walk by night were concerned. There was no denying he did seem uncommonly jumpy, but maybe it was just the noise he'd been making. The vague notion that Rufus might be taking his scaredness out on him was a new thought, though not a particularly comforting one.

'You were dreaming, that's all,' said Rufus, robustly, as if to refute the idea, 'you're in a funk over nothing. Soldiers aren't frightened of dreams. Just as well you're not advancing with bayonet drawn under a creeping barrage. You'd be a hopeless blob of jelly with bayonet drawn under a creeping barrage.'

But he didn't say it with anything more than customary superiority, so Adam knew he was forgiven for having let the side down squealing in his sleep, and anyway Nanny didn't seem to have heard. He scrambled out of bed and went over to the window with his brother, and together they watched the morning climb over Cutcombe Hill.

'It's going to be set fair today,' said Rufus. 'Let's have a boat race. You can be Oxford.'

This was charitable of him since Oxford was the family university. Whenever they normally had a boat race, Adam was Cambridge as a matter of course.

As the light brightened and the nightmare receded, it became less and less important to tell Rufus the full details of the dream. There didn't seem any point, he could hardly remember it himself. Only a line from the hymn they'd sung in church last Sunday and which the Reverend Biddle had preached upon, came to him, 'They fly forgotten as a dream dies at the opening day.'

Just one thing remained perfectly clear in his memory, refusing to die like the opening day or the rabbit they'd run over in the car coming back from tea with the Warrenders at Combe Withiel, running about the road, screaming.

In his dream, the figure in the bed had been his father.

112

PART TWO

1

By dint of frenzied exertion, and with the aid of a wide but shallow ditch, by darting across, and very often into, a handy terrain of marsh, Tristram had managed to evade the dogs and the pursuers, and he now travelled more moderately, lying up by day and creeping across country, avoiding all roads and habitations, during the brief hours of darkness.

He was now desperately hungry. His only food had been a turnip or two he had found in a derelict barn, his only water hurried gulps from streams and cattle-troughs that tasted of tinctured urine.

He felt desperately like giving up, abandoning himself to the hands of the first person who stopped him, it could easily be someone who would put him in touch with the Resistance, but he knew he couldn't risk it, he had to keep on and find the cave with the transmitter whose location was so imprinted on his mind, because the lives of others, conceivably a whole army depended on him. And so he drove himself forward like Poor Tom, through hedgerow and thicket, across meadow and copse, plunging here through a river and there through dense forest, on and on to where he knew the operator was waiting for him.

Tonight he was in luck. He had stumbled across what was clearly some kind of allotment in which he could see, by the light of the quarter moon, rows of carrot and radishes and even gooseberries wagging at him in orderly rows beseeching to be eaten.

Normally he might have avoided such a place as being too dangerous, guarded by a yokel with shotgun and dog in some adjacent hovel, but he could see no sign of any building, and now he rushed forward, clawing frantically at the ground, cramming leaves and roots and bits of earth into his mouth as he went. He progressed along the rows for a little like a yahoo, scrabbling and crouching backwards, until suddenly the universe stopped as he felt a sharp jab in his back.

He froze, the bile churning in his stomach along with a number of less definable ingredients.

Visions of hayforks in his kidneys, the firing squad and torture-chamber flitted through his mind as he waited for the guttural interrogation of his captor.

He hadn't felt like this since he was caught by the bushynosed Maths master reading *Health & Efficiency* behind his desk during prep, only even the Maths master (who had cut off one of his retreats by marrying the nurse from the school infirmary) couldn't beat him with rubber truncheons or attach electrodes to his sexual organs.

He could feel his mind quiet somewhere backstage, but up in front his body was blubbering with fear, the iron control, which the Son of Cutcombe could normally have expected to be able to call on, gone absent.

(Everything these last few days had been in fact like this, a deranged dream suffused with, as now, highlit moments, and then swallowed up again in a dark shadowiness shot through with leaves and barbed wire and brambles and sallows hitting you in the face as you ran.)

Slowly, very slowly, he turned. The gun in his back was unwavering. It felt more like a rifle than a shotgun but he couldn't say which he would have preferred.

'Please . . . don't . . . ' he could hear himself babbling. 'S'il vous plaît . . . Kamerad . . . '

And then suddenly he was laughing and sobbing and beating the ground with his fists.

It wasn't a gun in his back after all. It was the end of an old rake. And the figure wasn't a German soldier. A line from Tennyson came to his mind proving that a sound education is invaluable at times of breakdown.

'Birds in the garden calling "Maud, Maud, Maud",' the English master had said. 'What birds do you think the poet was referring to, youth?'

The thing was a bloody scarecrow.

2

'Here is the nine o'clock news on Saturday, August the 15th . . . bombers have successfully raided the Ruhr, reducing a number of key armaments factories to rubble. The city of Cologne is also reported to have sustained heavy damage . . .'

The morning sun streamed merrily into the small kitchen where Griselda and Franco sat smoking Craven As and drinking the last of the coffee which Mrs Sanderson had somewhat ostentatiously unearthed and donated (a little of) to her evacuees. The peaceful scene was interrupted by an unexpectedly violent gesture from her usually self-contained husband, as he reached across and brusquely switched off the wireless. Griselda was surprised. He had never shown more than passing interest in the conduct of the hostilities, saying the whole thing was simply a matter of little boys playing with penis substitutes. What is a rifle, he would say, but a smoking phallus? What is a gun but a stinkhorn? Now she thought fit to question him. His irritation usually meant one thing.

'What's the matter, Franco? Lost money on something?'

'Monsters. Those Americans. They are the Huns. That was beautiful cathedral in Cologne. Their bottoms are too big.'

'So was St Paul's.'

117

'Big bottom?'

'Cathedral, idiot. You didn't complain when the Germans dropped bombs on St Paul's.'

'St Paul's is good for English. But Wren, Wren is not Bernini. Wren suit the English mentality like . . . like Lyons Corner house.'

'Wren was a genius. Wren was beautiful. At least he finished St Paul's. Bernini was forever tinkering . . . '

'Is not important, Griselda mia. Is just . . . my mother was born in Köln.'

Griselda was surprised at this piece of information. Franco rarely imparted details of his background.

'I thought she was Italian.'

'She married Italian.'

'But that makes you . . . half-German . . . '

'Yes, yes. Do I have horns? Do I have cloven hoofs and eat babies?'

'I don't know, Franco, I really don't know. It just makes you a little madder than I thought. Does anyone else here know?'

'Why should they? I am Italian artist. You are still at war with me if I am German artist.'

'I just think you ought to tell someone, that's all. You might be in trouble if they found out.'

Franco leant over and gripped her hand, hard.

'Ow.'

'You tell no one, Griselda, you hear. This is for you and me.'

'You're hurting me.'

'You tell no one, Griselda.'

'All right, all right, I tell no one.'

Franco relaxed his grip leaving a reddening weal on her forearm, as he started to talk about the picture he was finishing. Everything seemed normal enough but a shadow had undeniably passed, and a little bit of it seemed, try as she might to shake it off, to have elected to stay, squatting like a toad at the corner of her attention.

3

Nanny had missed her period.

As she sloshed the thin milk (the top went into the great
wide jorums in the buttery ready for making into Cutcombe
cream for downstairs) she was busy counting. Thirty-one,
thirty-two, thirty-three . . . It was never as long as this, she
was regular as the grandfather clock on the stairs, yet still
she couldn't bring herself to take in the meaning of the
situation. She hated her period normally, it seemed such a
waste of time, but now she would give anything to see blood
on the sheet again. Babies happened to other people.

'Nanny?'

Bother the children, couldn't they leave a girl in peace?
She wanted to picture Rodgers again, the forbidden scent
of her body on his mouth, though, now she came to think
about it, even that made her feel queasy.

'What is it now?'

'If it's bacon for next course with eyes in it, can I leave it
for the starving children again?'

Bacon was one of the last things she wanted to think of,
last of all the bacon Queenie sent upstairs, specially cold
and greasy for the children, and tasting rankly of dead pig.
She hoped she wasn't going to start feeling unwell.

'No you could not. You'll eat every bit of it. I'm sick of
you and your faddy ways. If you don't eat it for breakfast,
you'll have it cold for lunch. And if you don't eat it for
lunch, you'll have it colder still for tea. And so on and so on
until it gets up and walks into your mouth. It's time you
little brats realized there's a war on.'

The boys were both shocked at her outburst, for Nanny
was normally, if not exactly good-tempered, at least too lazy
to be waspish, and it was generally agreed that the bacon,

119

underdone, fatty, and speckled with those ominous little white pimples of bone, was exempt from normal nursery eating laws.

'But . . . ' Adam's lip trembled.

He knew he'd be sick if he had to eat it, and he didn't want to be sick so early in the morning, but as it turned out, it was Nanny who was sick, very suddenly, into the waste-paper basket.

4

Julia was lying in late.

She was not normally an early riser even on such a flamboyantly glorious morning as this, but today she felt consumed with a more than conventional reluctance to cast aside the sheets.

'Cast care aside, lean on thy Guide.'

The words of the hymn came dimly back to her across the agnostic abyss of the last ten years (she could seldom be induced to attend the Reverend Biddle's services even for social reasons). But the religious zeal of the nuns at St Mary's, Kingham, where she had been at school for five years, had left their mark, though she was nearly expelled for wantonly cutting down an apple tree, and had been described by her Form Mistress as 'irretrievably light-weight'.

'Seek and His mercies will provide.'

The trouble was, she had no guide to lean on. She could hardly expect the Almighty, whatever the Bible might say about lost sheep, after so much neglect to come rushing up and tender an alleviating shoulder, and anyway her dilemma was hardly the sort of thing he would care to help resolve. The winds and tides, the Pope's ticklish situation vis à vis the German Catholics, the millions of extra souls to gather from concentration camp, city rubble and battle-field, to say nothing of the usual intake, the celibacy of the clergy, the long-delayed offensive against Hell, he certainly had his hands full, she felt, and could not be counted on to rally round and sort out the question as to whether or not she was going to offer her body to Thomas Lippincott. God would merely tut-tut and continue sorting out the sheep from the goats.

The trouble was, almost for the first time in her life, apart from a charming though painful episode when she was sixteen, she felt the ghost of an inkling that she was about to fall in love. The man touched her.

It was ridiculous, she knew.

Thomas was not her type at all. He was not rich, he was not particularly good-looking, he was not fashionable, he was not full of easy jokes and banter, or the light insults that sit so insouciantly on the lips of the Old Etonian. No, he was definitely bookish. It was impossible that she should be in love with a bookworm, that she should actually dream of making riotous love with him.

'You'd only know a good fuck if it came in a Harrods bag,' someone had said to her once, some disappointed Lothario thinking it would be an insult, an older man who had taken her out when she was only just eighteen, and who on a happier (and earlier) occasion had remarked it was like going out with one of the prizes before it was awarded.

How far he had been from knowing her. His insult had no barb. The act of sex itself she regarded coolly, sometimes pleasant, sometimes tiresome, like other people's cooking. She could take it or she could leave it. The important part was what it did to men. For her, it was a path to power, a means of keeping her minions on the lead, hopping and twitching to the tug of her body. 'Come along now, Alex, Jamie, Christopher, Algie, time for walkies.'

She rejoiced in the fact that sex left her largely unmoved, and whether she was good at it or not was of considerable unimportance to her.

'You don't have to eat the fox to enjoy the Hunt,' she used to say.

What a fortunate escape she had had from the obsession that appeared to hold the larger part of mankind in its grip, eternally tormenting themselves that they were having too little, doing it wrong or simply being hopelessly inadequate.

Of course if it came in a Harrods bag, it would be better. She might even be able to tolerate it with Fortnum & Mason on the label. What her ertswhile suitor had signally failed to grasp was that she could possibly feel insulted at such a suggestion. What did he think she would pride herself on enjoying: sex à la Woolworths?

She would look at herself sometimes, naked in the mirror, examining the breasts that made strong men gasp, the beguilingly forthcoming nipples, the firm belley seemingly unmarked by two bouts of childbearing (which of course she thought about as little as possible), the immaculately proportioned legs crowned with a delicate geometry of soft dark hair, and sometimes lying back she would explore intently those areas that had wrought such havoc among the hunting classes.

To be sure, she thought, it wasn't much to look at – and yet as she had regarded the brutishness of those unmakeupable features, catching sight as she did so of the perfection of her face, she thought it was somehow right that one should have that other blind face down there mocking away, sidelong and so completely and indelicately unlike one.

She put her hand, almost without thinking, down to it now, and was surprised to find a dampness there.

'Oh Thomas.'

It was all most disturbing. Really, this wasn't her at all.

She would have to let him do what he wanted, but it was going to be dreadfully inconvenient. She wasn't by any means certain that she was going to be in control of the situation. Should she? Shouldn't she? Even now, it still wasn't too late. She could call a halt to the whole thing, and carry on as she had always done, a lovely carrot for the donkeys.

'Oh Thomas, No.'

But the other mouth, the one that had responded obediently for so long, had discovered a mind of its own, and was giving an unequivocal affirmative.

The whole thing seemed to be out of her hands. Or in them, of course, depending on how you looked at it.

'Oh Thomas. Thomas darling . . .'

The breakfast gong, with its pecularly dismal sound, like a buoy on some illimitable stretch of estuary being agitated by the passing of the Flying Dutchman, boomed out in the hall below, but its summons fell on ears even deafer than Chell's.

Thomas was experiencing his apotheosis, and he wasn't even there.

5

Chell's ears were turned down as far as they could go, as it happened, because the Granny was eating cornflakes, prunes and clotted cream with a relentless succulence that made you wish you were dead. It had a terrible beam-like quality that had begun to penetrate Chell's aural senses in a way that gave her alternative hope and despair. She swore that the Granny, properly lined up with spoon and porringer outside the walls of Jericho, would have made both Joshua with his trumpet, and the host of Israel with its mighty shout, form up at the Labour Exchange for alternative employment.

'One day,' thought Chell, 'one day I'm going to tell her. One day she'll go too far and I won't be able to stop myself. Cutcombe this and Cutcombe that. I'll give her Cutcombe where it hurts.'

She would too, because pottering in the garden a couple of weeks ago near where Ferdy Fowler made the bonfires, she had spotted a letter lying beside the path. Already torn, no doubt consigned to the rubbish bin, it must have fallen off the refuse cart on the way to Ferdy's ghat.

It was a letter from Tristram to the simpering dame down at the stables proving beyond doubt that the Son of Cutcombe had feet of clay, and it provided Chell with just the sort of ammunition she had been praying for.

For two weeks she had sat through the Grandmother's habitual homilies and self-congratulations hugging the secret to her thin bosom. For two weeks, she had lain in her bed in the darkness, chuckling herself to sleep.

'BOH!'

A sound like a howitzer roused her from her reverie.

She looked about her, blinking and clutching at her flat chest. It was the Grandmother, of course, who unnoticed by Chell had reached across the table to turn her volume up again. She was now laughing heartily at her little prank. Chell sat dazedly as the coffee pots and the plates and the marmalade and the earthenware pots of Cutcombe butter assembled on the tablecloth again, and the portrait of the boys on the wall reassumed its kilter.

'Never turn your twangling instrument right down, Chell. You might miss something important . . . an air-raid warning, perhaps . . . or one of our bons mots. Cutcombe has always been noted for its conversation. I remember James Barrie used to say when he came down . . . '

Chell glowered at her, mumbling something about conservation of batteries.

They hadn't heard an air-raid warning up here since the war started, but there was no point in remonstrance. It would be much more satisfying to speak out, to say the things she had been saving and saving until they seethed like molten lava, putting unendurable pressures on her brainpan.

'I turned it off before you moved on to crunching toast, which is a sound so appalling I'm recommending it to the War Office for use in the interrogation of prisoners, if they agree to swop it for a landmine in your rockery. As for your precious son, he's a fraud, a coward and a lecher, and I'm going to make you get down on your knees and crawl if you want to stop me telling the West Somerset Free Press,' she wanted to say, but though the temptation was intense, she knew the time wasn't right.

She wanted to think about it a little more first. She would go for a walk and think about it a little more first. It was a lovely day for a gloat.

'I think I'll take a walk over to Luxborough this afternoon,' she said, innocently, 'that is, if you haven't got anything you want me to do.'

'Certainly I have, certainly I have as you very well know. There's the WVS jumble sale correspondence, and the minutes for the next meeting of the Land Army Welfare Committee . . . I doubt, I very much doubt . . . ' here she peered at her watch and looked grave, an expression somewhat marred by over-vigorous mastication, 'if we'll be finished by lunchtime.'

'To see how Ivy Bassett's getting on, I mean.'

That was clever of her, Ivy, one of the parlour maids, although over fifty, kept having phantom pregnancies and was a source of some concern at Cutcombe.

'Aye me, aye me. If ye must, ye must. You may take her some of last year's goosegog jam. Be sure to tell her it's

125

from me. Poor silly old Ivy.'

Poor silly old Ivy having already mislaid her mind and by now a goodly family of foetuses would in that case no doubt lose her teeth as well, Chell reflected, since last year's batch of gooseberry jam had not come up to Cutcombe standard and, being adhesive as nougat, had to be disposed of among the sugar-starved villagers. Another candidate for her sales-drive in Whitehall, she thought. The Air Ministry this time. Cutcombe goosegog could be the perfect window fixative for night fighters – or, for that matter, day.

'Thinking of going to the party tonight, Chell?'

She sensed danger, and acted absent-minded, as if listening to unseen voices.

'The party?'

'Down at the Camp, duffer.'

The last thing she wanted to do was be jostled by those noisy Americans, swilling beer and eating doughnuts and telling her about their home towns in Idaho. She played safe.

'I don't think I've been asked.'

'Nonsense. We're all asked.'

Curses. The old hag wasn't going to announce her intention of attending?

On thinking about it more, though, Chell saw through the ruse. Apart from the Morris dancing, the Grandmother could have not the slightest wish to go unless she, Chell, made her distaste for the occasion known. She would then, putting her own age and disinclination aside, pronounce her determination to be present herself, with Chell in mandatory attendance.

Chell acted swiftly, smiling with spinsterly raffishness.

'In that case, I think I might go and hah! cut a rug.'

'I'm sorry, Chell. I'm afraid I'm rather counting on your services here this evening, specially if you're going to be out all afternoon.'

Chell put her napkin back into its ivory ring, and rose

from the table feeling well pleased with the morning's work.

6

Major Chuck was sitting in his office assisting the war effort by lightly massaging the inside knee of Private Estelle Ruffels, but he put her down gamely when Thomas entered, and addressed himself to business.

'See here,' he said, dispensing with pleasantries, 'see here ah Lieutenant.'

Thomas saw there and stood looking at it for some time while Major Chuck tapped an obbligato on his teeth with his propelling pencil. Private Ruffels, perched on the edge of the desk with pad at the ready, took up the Second Percussion part with her stenographer's HB Venus. Thomas had the impression he'd met the scene before in somebody else's account of the incident.

He had no idea why he had been summoned to the Major's office, but the drift so far suggested that it was to give his views on a mooted riff-oriented office-equipment musical cabaret for the evening's festivities, no doubt to follow hot on the heels of the West Somerset Mummers. Though not over-enthusiastic about the performance, he thought it showed originality so he gave it a modest benediction.

'Yes,' he said, 'I see. Very interesting. I like it.'
Major Chuck's normally florid complexion swelled to a rich mulberry.

'What the hell are you talking about, Lippincott?'

'The cabaret, sir. The pencils.'

'Are you trying to make a monkey out of me?'

Private Ruffels had stopped tapping and was now sucking. She opened her eyes very wide and looked interestedly at Thomas.

'Me, sir. No, sir.'

Private Ruffels crossed her legs prodigiously.

'Disturbing, Lieutenant,' said the Major.

'Definitely, sir,' said Thomas, looking at the legs and feeling unfaithful.

'Read it, you idiot,' said the Major.

Thomas saw that the Major was holding a flimsy telegram form towards him. It was headed TOP SECRET.

'BRITISH INTELLIGENCE SUSPECT ENEMY AGENT OPERATING CAMP LOCALITY. EXERCISE MAXIMUM VIGILANCE. REPORT SUSPICIOUS PERSONNEL. BROBDINGNAG,' he read.

'You Camp Intelligence Officer?' said the Major.

'Acting Camp Intelligence Officer, sir.'

'You Camp Intelligence Officer or not?'

'Yes, sir. But . . .'

But, he was going to add, he didn't know anything about locating enemy agents. It was all he could do to locate a 16mm version of *Gone with the Wind* for the next Base Film Night. And who the hell was Brobdingnag? Or was it some kind of cryptic instruction?

The Major, however, had no time for others' self-doubts.

'But nothing. You're the Intelligence Officer and I'm the officer in charge of the Intelligence Officer in this camp and I'm telling you, Lieutenant, get Intelligent. Eyes wide. Ears to the ground. Get the picture?' Major Chuck mimed elaborately just in case Thomas had missed some finer point. 'Back here 1600 hours with your report. The British are sending someone down tomorrow and he'll want to read it. And *I'll* want to have time to read it first. OK?'

'But . . .'

But, he was going to say, I've arranged to meet the most beautiful woman in the world at 1600 hours for a picnic. Fortunately, he had learned to develop a sense of self-preservation in the Army.

'Whaddya say? But? BUT?'

'No, no, Major. The butts. The er shooting range up behind the Old Quarry . . .' his brain raced like a weasel. 'I thought when I was up there a couple of weeks ago giving a talk on prophylaxis to the men, between firing, I thought I saw a suspicious-looking guy disappearing into the woods. I thought I might go up later and look around. After, uh, looking around here first.'

The range was only a mile from where he had fixed to meet her.

The Major nodded cumbrously as the import of what Thomas was saying hopped across his frontal lobes, neuron to neuron, like an old tramp crossing a river.

'Very well, then, Lieutenant. But report to me as soon as you get back.'

'Yes, sir.'

'Remember we have a party here this evening, so I want you back in good time. No skulking off to a certain hospitable house in these parts, right?'

'Right.'

'And remember, Lieutenant. Leave no stone unturned.'

'It'd be difficult in a quarry.'

'What was that?'

Private Ruffels opened her eyes very wide again and gave Thomas a disgraceful wink.

7

Tristram had discontinued his plunge across country at first light, as he had done in countless training exercises, and had found a burrow in a deserted haybarn on the edge of a copse of great oaks that clustered round the base of an escarpment. The whole place looked astonishingly English, almost as though he had been here before, rather than a random and unlooked-for corner of a foreign field, but he was too tired to ruminate further.

In spite of his fatigue, however, he couldn't sleep. His mind seethed with thoughts and images which kept bobbing up to the surface like old bones in a bouillon, and then slowly sinking again to be replaced by other half-fleshed ragged memories. The chicken's dinner bucket, that's what his mind was, like the one Queenie used to have on the Aga full of mysterious swirling shapes, leftovers and old potatoes which, when he was small, he thought smelled better than the nursery lunch, especially when the bran was mixed in and Ferdy Fowler let him mash it. And then he would go out to the chicken-run, take the stick out of the egg-box latch, and cautiously feel inside for the eggs, fearful of irritable beaks.

'Go arn, 'ee won't peck 'ee,' Ferdy Fowler would say if one of the broody Rhode Islands was still in possession, and Tristram would slip his hand underneath and pull out the egg, so warm you'd think it'd be cooked.

'Look, Ferdy, I did it.'

'Well done, Master Tristram. Now 'ee go and do it to Marmaduke.'

Marmaduke was the ferocious gander who attacked everything regardless of size or species, and had once been seen scaring the daylights out of a fox. It was a little joke between Ferdy and himself, because once Marmaduke had chased him right across Six Acre when he had incautiously gone mushrooming one morning, and Ferdy would never tire of trotting it out when they went to get the eggs.

'Now 'ee do it to Marmaduke. Huh huh huh . . . 'Eed have your fingers like chiperlarters.'

'You're not frightened of him, are you, Ferdy?'

He couldn't quite understand what Ferdy was doing in Brittany but it didn't worry him too much. Ferdy had a way of suddenly appearing out of the trees, old sack round his shoulders, trousers so faded and grubby you couldn't tell what their original colour might have been, done up with string and bagging down in massive folds like a Turk's.

'Frightened? Lor bless you, no, Master Tristram, I'm not frightened of dying. Dying's nothing. It's the thought of having my fingernails torn out makes me fidgety. It's the rubber tube. And having my balls used as electric light bulbs . . . '

'Ferdy?'

A small brown rat ran among the shadows, pausing to preen itself in a sliver of sunlight.

'Ferdy?'

He must've slipped into the trees again. Good of him to make it. He couldn't go far wrong if Ferdy was keeping an eye on him. Tonight, he thought as the tiredness finally closed over him, tonight I should just about get there. Then I can go home.

Taunton, Norton Fitzwarren, Bishop's Lydeard, Stogumber, Crowcombe, Watchet, Blue Anchor, Washford, Dunster, and up into the hills in the Wolseley Eighteen Six.

131

8

HMS *Eagle* and HMS *Manchester* had been lost on the Malta Convoy, the Germans were storming through the Caucasus like nobody's business, rape, pillage, distress and banditry weevilled their way through the cradles of Western civilization, but the high woods of Cutcombe remained unperturbed, and the pigeons sang 'My toe bleeds, Betty' (at least that's what the Granny said they sang) with a loopy lovesickness that made a complete nonsense of the war effort.

Up on the rounded sides of Cutcombe Hill, corn ripened to a deep blond, hanging its locks down seemingly-impossible slopes to tease the harvester, hiding among its trammels a Doone-like population of robber rabbits.

Further along, towards the Common, green bracken from stream to summit fizzed with insects, plaguing the ponies and deer which strayed over from Exmoor way, and goading the unwary walker to slice his hand on the stalks as he pulled desperately for a fan to switch the creatures away.

But nearer home, along the bottom of the valley, the Cutcombe River rattled along between mossy-green banks and bellying boulders, and here the boys played at stepping-stones as they walked in the striped hot and cool of the morning after breakfast.

'Bet I see a trout before you do,' said Rufus, competitive as ever.

'I don't mind if you do,' said Adam, skipping over a branch that forked out from the bank like a rusty snake. 'Anyway I just saw one.'

'Liar.'

'I did.'

'Where?'

Adam hadn't seen one, and he really couldn't imagine why he'd said that he had. It was quite unnecessary. But now he'd done it, he couldn't go back on the lie. Why was Rufus always so keen to demolish him, like the way he'd demolished him this morning when he'd reduced his forces before breakfast to just Colonel Green and a broken field gun, and no doubt when they came to have the boat race, Cambridge would win for the first time in history?

'Under that rock,' he said, without great conviction.

'It's in the shade there. You couldn't possibly have seen it.'

'I jolly well did. It was a big one too.'

'All right, then. Lie down and tickle it.'

The river was shallow for the most part, but it had pools where the boulders dammed it, deep enough to swim in, if you could swim: Nanny said you had to be careful if you didn't want to come a cropper.

Adam nearly came a cropper now as a piece of slippery moss sheared off as he edged over. Why had he started this?

'Look out, stupid,' said Rufus, confident of triumph.

The water, toasted along the shallow bed further up the valley, was warm under the rock, and he watched his arm appear to fracture as it went below the surface.

'Look. I've got a broken arm.'

But Rufus was not to be deflected.

'Come on. You're wasting time.'

Time seemed to be there to be wasted, an infinite reservoir like the heat off the water, shimmering on and on, or like Granny's still-room, a spicy mine of unlimited supplies, but Adam knew better than to argue, and addressed himself once more to the matter in hand.

He could feel Rufus right behind him, knowing there were no trout there, driving him to the limits of his lie, and he plunged his arm into the depths right up to the short

133

sleeves of his Aertex shirt, groping the clammy belly of the boulder but coming up with nothing but weed.

.'You're a liar. There's nothing there. You know what we do to liars.'

Adam made another attempt as Rufus crowed gloatingly above him, and as he did so he felt, or thought he felt, a horrible slimy something, limp but vicious, reach out and clutch at his hand under the rock.

He yelled, slipped, recovered and fell, pulling Rufus down with him.

The water was deceptively deep, five or six feet at least, and neither of them could really swim. Rufus had achieved a few strokes of dog-paddle at Blue Anchor, but Adam simply scrabbled and sank unless the man with the gym belt tied to the hockey-stick at Minehead Baths was there to hoick him along.

Here, caught unawares, with clothes and shoes on, in fresh water, and clutched at by Adam, even Rufus's rudimentary skills failed him. As Adam bobbed up, he was aware of his brother floundering furiously and making noises of distress — which he was bound to deny later — if there was going to be a later.

Strangely enough, he didn't feel frightened, the water was so clear and warm, brown at the bottom and swirly around him, like being inside a glass marble. As his heart raced, it seemed as though everything else slowed down. The darting minnows seemed caught in aspic, and he looked down on them fascinated, remembering the drought they'd had last summer and how he'd actually paddled in this very same pool.

And then he came up to the surface again, and everything was happening very fast.

'Whooooph.'

Up on the top he became terrified. He realized he was shouting. There was a buzzing in his ears and his throat tasted of river. Rufus was lost in a thrashing of spray

134

somewhere over to the right.

'Woroworoooof.'

He sank into the marble once more. Captain or was it Major Marble? It was calm down here. He was locked inside the swirliness of greens and browns, and he wasn't in the least bit scared, not of the water anyway, though when he came to think of the hand and who it belonged to, and mysteriously there was time to think of everything now, it did become more worrying, though he didn't even know if it was a hand or just something he'd imagined — he was always imagining things like that, hands coming up under the bedclothes at the bottom, cold hands smelling of river, to grab his feet.

Perhaps it was a Fright. Hadn't there been a sort of froggy fishy one?

He didn't quite understand why they should come for him by day, though perhaps under water counted as night, but in a way he was glad they'd finally launched their attack. He wouldn't have to worry about them any more, he could just sit in his marble and forget about everything.

When he came up for the third time, he was weaker — but still capable of surprise when he saw that Rufus had now managed to extricate himself from the water, and was sitting negligently on a rock wringing his shirt out.

This seemed to him such a black-hearted act of abandonment and treachery, to say nothing of careless-ness, that he forgot his terror and became indignant. How could anyone attend to their laundry when someone was so obviously drowning right in front of their ugly mugs?

He opened his mouth to protest, took a mighty swig of Cutcombe river water, sank, twirled in the marble, passed out, and awoke to find himself on the river bank lying stomach down, being pummelled by strong hands that didn't seem quite to know what they were doing.

'Time like an ever-rolling stream bears all his sons away,' a voice which he did not at first recognize remarked.

He sat up, spewed out a small quantity of river water in which there were no minnows, though he looked to see, and discovered that the voice (and hands) belonged to the American Lieutenant who came to visit and walked along the upper stream, talking about the Monstrous Crow.

'At least, it didn't quite make it this time, bear you away, I mean. Are you OK? It's lucky I heard you yelling. Even then I thought you were just fooling around. Didn't anyone ever tell you water's hard to breathe?'

Thomas was more upset than the boys were, and didn't care to think what might have happened if he hadn't decided to make a little detour near the house on his way to see the Range Warden (so he wouldn't have to do it this afternoon). Accidents, he thought, never quite seem like part of life, more as if they've crept in from somewhere disorderly, under the door.

The boys considered his question, moistly, recovering from the ordeal as quickly as dogs. They had, of course, been told not to play near the pools, but Rufus never took that kind of suggestion very seriously.

'As for you,' said the Lieutenant, turning his attention to the elder boy, 'it's not very nice letting your brother drown while you address yourself to your toilette.'

Rufus's white face broke into a smile.

'I was only trying to teach him to swim,' he said, 'he'll never learn if he depends on a harness. Granny always says the only way my Father learned to swim was being thrown in at the deep end.'

Thomas had not met the Son of Cutcombe, simply envying him in absentia, but he spared him a moment of solicitude.

'That's about the craziest thing I ever heard. Learning to swim's a serious business. It's for grownups to teach. You can't go around pitching people into the water and hoping they'll float. Understand? Drowning can be fatal. So cut it out, will you?'

Thomas was considerably upset. The situation was hopelessly out of hand down this part of the river.

'All right. I'm sorry.'

The child appeared contrite.

'Fine. Fine. Just don't do it any more. There's enough people getting killed these days without you kids joining in.'

Speaking of the war reminded him of the object of his visit.

'You haven't seen any suspicious-looking strangers around here, have you? Anyone who might be nosing around?'

'Strangers?'

'I don't know. Just anyone, I guess.'

'There's never anyone much round here. Just Rodgers and Ferdy Fowler. And even they don't come up here much. Then there's Franco, of course.'

Franco. He hadn't thought of the Italian Sardonicus.

'He's all over the place. Painting mostly.'

Of course. One wouldn't expect a painter to confine himself to his quarters.

'No one else, hm? No Monstrous Owls?'

Adam was going to tell him about his dream but stopped just in time when he saw the look on Rufus's face.

'OK. Well. I guess I'd better be off.'

'What were you doing here yourself?

The elder brother's question could, Thomas felt, have been put more charmingly, in view of the results of his appearance, but he supposed he did have a point.

'Just taking the scenic route up to the range. Maybe see you later.'

He turned to follow the path.

'You OK now, Adam?'

Adm considered. The warmth of the sun seemed to have dried out the whole experience, like the water in his shirt, leaving only a vanishing smudge on the rock. He nodded, handed back the coat Thomas had put round his shoulders, and did a little dance on the grass.

'How's your mother?' Thomas asked.

'Very well, thank you. Very well, thank you.'

'Please give her my regards.'

'Yes we will. Yes we will.'

Rufus, as usual, was more practical.

'You won't tell anyone about it, will you? I mean the swimming lesson.'

Thomas was momentarily mortified. He had hoped he might tell their Mother, who would be duly impressed and love him all the more, but he had the impression that, if the Grandmother heard of it, retribution would be painful.

'OK. But see here. Just don't do it again.'

'We won't. We promise.'

As Thomas trudged away up the valley, Rufus turned almost kindly to Adam.

'You blithering idiot. You nearly had us all in the soup.'

And they ran about naked in the sun.

Somewhere, far out on the Bristol Channel, target practice started, the woolly rumble of the guns only adding to the sensations of peace.

'He's potty,' said Rufus, 'he's talking to himself.'

But Thomas was quoting again.

> 'On the idle hill of summer,
> Sleepy with the flow of streams,
> Far I hear the distant drummer
> Drumming like a noise in dreams.'

9

Griselda, sitting at the bottom of the steps that led down from the flat into the stableyard, a pile of pea-pods lying half-shelled beside her in the sun, was trying to reconcile the feeling of well-being induced by the heat with a sense of perplexity bordering on dismay evoked by her situation. Married to her inscrutable alien, living on someone else's charity (someone else she didn't much care for), having an unsatisfactory affair with the married son of the very woman who was handing out the largesse, she could not think of any particular reason for feeling buoyant. The sun was certainly very nice, but she had a sense of creeping shadows that had nothing to do with the state of the morning.

She went over her problems in a little more detail. Franco, for instance. She didn't feel she wanted to ask him where he slipped off to for his long nocturnal rambles. There was talk of Peggy in the village, who had been known to distribute favours, but Peggy, if Peggy it was, could only be a minor peccadillo simply serving to remind her of what she knew already: that Franco wasn't going to remain married to her or quite possibly to anyone for very long. He simply needed her for the duration of hostilities.

For some time, the practical side of her nature had been coming to terms with this notion. It had encouraged her to embark on her affair. But what was she to do now? She still most regrettably wanted Franco, and yet she couldn't help beginning to want to leave him.

As for Tristram, she knew now he could never really be the answer for her; but she'd grown so used to having the comfortable cushion of his adulation behind her that it was with a considerable sense of irritation that she realized there had been no letter at the Dunster poste-restante now for nearly three weeks.

Had he fallen out of love with her? And, if he had, wasn't it rather a good thing? But why did she feel a slight sense of chill at this failure?

Maybe it was the stone steps of the stable stairs. Come, come, she thought, one must be sensible. She wriggled the rope mat under her buttocks, and applied herself once more to the pile of pods.

'Minding your peas and queue, Zelda? said the familiar voice.

Franco always had this extraordinary knack of turning up when you weren't expecting, making you fluster and hide your mind. She gave a start, and the pod she was shelling discharged its cargo across the courtyard, peas scuttling like naughty thoughts between the paving-stones.

'What a lucky little mat to have such a nice queue sitting on it. If you like you can use my face.'

'That's not funny, Franco. It's absolutely disgusting. You confirm all the Englishman's worst fears about the latin races. And don't try and make out you find me attractive when you sneak off wherever you go night after night.'

'But Zelda, you know I find it difficult to sleep. I must think about my work, about what is happening to my country. It is only at night that such things can be ordered.'

'All right, then. Where do you go?'

'I tell you, Zelda. I wander like the Miller,' he hummed a snatch of Schubert, 'I wander, as you say, up hill and down dale. More down dale than up hill if I can find those damn dales. Too many damn hills round here.'

'I don't believe you, Franco.'

'What?'

'You see, I followed you.'

140

Franco's face grew dark and Griselda momentarily quailed.

'You follow me, huh? My wife follow me? So now you know the secret, huh?'

She had not expected him to take the accusation so grimly. She could have sworn he would laugh and brazen it out — or even admit it and talk about the artist's needs.

'No, no,' she was quick to let herself off the hook. 'That's just what I don't know. Otherwise I wouldn't ask. I lost you in the dark.'

Franco seemed much relieved at this, but the whole conversation was beginning to negate the cordial effects of the rush-matting. Why was he so disturbed? Was it more than a carnal affair? Was he actually in love with someone? She wouldn't have thought it possible. It couldn't conceivably be Peggy, but who else was there? It would be too much of a joke if it were the boys' mother up at the Hall.

But Franco didn't seem to think he was within a hundred miles of a jest. He looked over her sombrely.

'Never follow me again, Zelda. Understand? If you do, it means finito, right? I am an artist . . . '

Ah, there it was. Suddenly everything was all right again. He had found his poise, and was pushing out smoke like a surprised (but not damaged) destroyer.

' . . . I must be free. I will not have women following me like dogs. If I choose to walk in the woods, that is my affair. If I choose to sleep with the little ragazza in the village, that is my affair too. You do not understand the artistic spirit, Zelda. You are provincial . . . '

She knew she ought to be angry but somehow she couldn't help laughing. It made her resent him all the more. He was impossible.

' . . . Where your soul ought to be you have an English pudding. Promise me now, down on your knees, you never do anything so provincial again.'

'I promise, Franco, but I won't go down on my knees because I'll spill the peas.'

The inadvertent rhyme amused him.

'Spill the peas, Zelda. After all, you have just spill the beans.'

'Do stop fooling, Franco. I've got things to do. Go and paint or something.'

'Promise me on your crumpet-faced mother.'

'I promise on my crumpet-faced mother.'

'Good. That is good. You are good girl, Zelda, even if you have a soul like a zuppa inglese.'

She could feel the anger and laughter rising within her like heartburn. She tried letting out a little rage.

'I wouldn't follow you again even if I hadn't promised. Don't you think it's a little humiliating for a wife, floundering about in the forest looking for your mistresses?'

She almost convinced herself that this was what she had done instead of peeping at his retreating figure from the cover of the stable wall.

'I can't think why I did it in the first place. Anyway, I'm glad you spelt out your theory of art and immorality being so inextricably connected. I'm thinking of taking up art myself as a matter of fact. Sauce for the gander and all that sort of thing.'

'Marmaduke?'

Each successive gander at Cutcombe was called Marmaduke, in the manner of the Pharaohs. This one was Marmaduke IV.

'Il Marmaduce? What has that that monster got to do with it. He is not gander, he is Eumenides. You cannot eat Eumenides. It would have the most fatal consequences.'

'I'm not talking about Marmaduke, Franco, I'm talking about Art.'

She did her best to maintain her wrath but it wasn't easy.

'Art? You have as much art as a Spotted Dick.'

'Maybe if I'm immoral enough it might improve.'

But Franco started to hum some impenetrable snatch of Puccini, which he usually did when he got tired of a subject.

At this moment, Chell, of all people, hove into view walking across the cobbled floor as if it were coming at her in waves. Finally making it to the steps, she stood before them scowling patiently while she lugged her deaf aid round to a position where she could operate the dials.

'What?' she said, finally, testing for volume, 'What? What? What? What ? WHAT?'

'Hullo,' said Griselda.

'Where? Which? When?' said Franco, unnecessarily, 'And Why?'

'Got something for you,' said Chell, 'found it in the potting shed. Thought it was a bit rum.'

'Do you mind speaking up?' said Franco.

'How kind of you,' said Griselda, kicking him. 'What is it?'

Chell rummaged in her cavernous bag, which swung down among the twangling instrument batteries like an ill-assorted bosom, and extracted a crumpled envelope.

'Here,' she said, thrusting it forth, 'it's addressed to you.'

Griselda realized with sinking sensations around the plexus that it was one of Tristram's envelopes. She always went to the potting shed to read, finding the mild mulchy atmosphere conducive to the softer emotions, besides being more withdrawn from common view. She must have dropped it on her last visit.

Clearly Chell had been playing the spy. She looked at her with mingled feelings of hatred and trepidation, waiting for the usual four sheets of Tristram's scribble to emerge.

Franco, never slow on the uptake, discerned a tenseness in her manner.

'Ha haaah,' he said, jocosely, 'so we have the secret communications. Let me inspect the document.'

He took the envelope from Chell's evil paw and peered into it briskly. Griselda's heart sank to her sensible shoes.

'There's nothing in it . . . now,' said Chell with a meaning look at Griselda, whose heart, baulked of its downward course, essayed a lurch sideways.

'Well, well. Arcanum est. Let us see. What do we know about it? It comes, yes, it comes from Grantham.' Franco perused the envelope as if it were a communication from the Sibyl herself.

'That's in Lincolnshire,' Chell put in swiftly.

'And somehow I recognize the writing. It is . . . no . . . not La Crumpetta . . . it is . . . Do you know whose it is, Miss Chelford?'

'What did he say?' said Chell, playing Franco at his own game.

'I SAY, DO YOU KNOW WHOSE IT IS?'

'No need to screech. You Italians are always screaming. Screech, screech, screech. It's all that shouting ICE-A-CREAMA. No. I couldn't say.'

Chell had somehow taken offence at Franco's manner, and decided to clam up. Griselda swallowed with relief. She hated rows and being found out. But what did the old witch want?

'So. We have to ask the recipient? Unfold the mystery, Zelda.'

'It's only a letter. Nothing mysterious about that.'

'Ah . . . but in the pottering shed. That is a naughty place to read letters. Especially when they are not addressed to you at home among the lares et penates.'

Franco had a point, but for a wild moment memories of childhood fibbing prompted her to deny that she'd ever received the thing, that it was all part of some elaborate practical joke or scurrilous plot calculated to impugn her honour, till she suddenly remembered some good advice she had once received on the subject of lying: when in doubt keep as near as possible to the truth.

'All right, then. It was from an old boyfriend. AN OLD BOYFRIEND,' she screeched for Chell's benefit.

Chell threw her another mutant foetus from her bag of pregnant glances and beat a retreat back across the gale-force pebbles.

'So Zelda. You are receiving other men's envelopes. And where is the wicked letter inside the naughty envelope?'

Griselda knew that Chell had tucked it away among the camphor ice, secateurs and jujubes deep within the recesses of her hold-all, but all she said was:

'The wicked dog ate it.'

'Zelda, you are becoming saucy,' said Franco.

'What is saucy for the gander is saucy for the goose,' she replied, feeling, for the first time that day, not entirely displeased with herself.

10

Cousins Lucy and Badger were coming to lunch, brought over from Taunton by their mother, Mrs Pilgrim, a spare and peevish woman related by some removes to Old Mr Sanderson.

It meant Rufus and Adam would be allowed down to lunch in the grownups' dining-room, a change in routine which Adam regarded with mixed feelings: the food would be better but the atmosphere more critical. Eyes down, mustn't gobble, don't speak unless you're spoken to (never with your mouth full), and waterworks with the gravy and mashed potato totally forbidden. These were the Standing Orders, and Granny would see that they were rigorously obeyed.

The party arrived at noon, and the grownups went into the library to drink a pre-prandial sherry.

'Why don't you take Lucy and Badger out to play in the garden?' someone said, predictably.

The notion that just because you were a child you would be bound to get on with other children had absolutely no foundation in experience or common sense, and therefore endeared itself particularly to adults. (Granny applied the same principle to foreigners — she had gone to enormous lengths to bring together two Poles in the vicinity, one of whom was an alcoholic atheist and the other a devout and aesthetic museum curator. The meeting had not been a success, but Granny had been too busy talking about Cutcombe tennis parties in the Old Days to notice the shudders of incompatibility.)

The children straggled out glumly into the garden.

Adam had not seen his cousins for over a year, and surveyed them without optimism as they crossed the drive and padded listlessly about on the lawn.

Badger who was really called Roger was large for his eight years with a tendency to podginess. He was a pale and bad-tempered child, no doubt taking after his mother, but even she wasn't given to tackling people low only five minutes after she'd met them, which was what he now did to the elder of his two cousins. Rufus looked livid, but being smaller than Badger, could offer little resistance, which encouraged his relative to pin his arm behind his back and demand that he beg for mercy.

'Actually, honestly,' said Rufus, which was the nearest Adam had ever heard him get to a submission.

Badger seemed temporarily appeased, produced a bat and ball from his mother's Morris 8, and led Rufus away by the ear towards a smooth stretch of lawn to play cricket, totally ignoring, to Adam's considerable relief, the two younger children. Badger, he felt, would play to maim.

He turned to say something to Cousin Lucy. He hadn't

met her when they last visited the Pilgrims — she had been in bed recovering from flu or something. It now turned out that his relative was beautiful.

She was perhaps the same age as he, but where he was mousy, she was a star, with rosebud mouth, periwinkle eyes and cheeks the colour of Ferdy Fowler's nectarines, the whole effect crowned with the softest and bubbliest of golden curls. Her simple dress, a blue frock with short puffy sleeves and white socks inside neat little blue sandals, merely served to heighten the effect.

She looked at him and smiled. It reminded him of the Reverend Biddle's story of the little Saxons brought before St Augustine. 'Non Angli sunt sed angeli.' He thought he knew how St Augustine must have felt — rather humble but bucked at the impact of such loveliness.

'Do you want to see my knickers?' she enquired.

Adam was only temporarily at a loss. It was true that no one had ever proffered quite such an unequivocal invitation before, but he had once been in love with a girl called Diana Davies who played the recorder and did wonderful cartwheels on Minehead Beach, and he had been so moved that the night he had stayed with the Davieses he had peed in his bed — the very last time it had ever happened. So knickers weren't altogether an undreamt-of area in his life. He had been stirred once by the sight of Diana's flying blue serge. He found himself being stirred again.

'Yes, please,' he said. 'Thank you very much indeed.'

He was a polite little boy.

She took him by the hand, and led him instinctively to the very best part of the shrubbery where nobody could possibly see them, looking back at him every now and then with a smile of urgent mischief.

'There,' she said. 'That's better. Now. Would you like to see front or back first?'

She had clearly done this before.

'Both,' said Adam.

His favourite attitude, his old nanny used to say, was sitting on the fence, having his cake and eating it.

'That's greedy,' said Lucy.

'Sorry,' said Adam.

'Least said, soonest mended,' said Lucy. 'Here you are, then.'

She lifted up her frock and displayed with some pride a jolly pair of light blue drawers with white flowers embroidered on them. Her navel positively twinkled with naughtiness. Adam felt a delicious guilt creeping upon him, giving his own pair of Doctor Deimal's thermal, problems quite beyond the designer's brief. Lucy turned and bent her bottom up towards him.

'It's nice, isn't it?' she said. 'Go on. Touch it.'

Adam stretched out a quivering hand and gingerly patted the cottony smoothness.

'Don't dab,' said Lucy. 'You can stroke it if you like.'

Adam stroked assiduously.

'And now,' said Lucy, 'let's see yours.'

'Mine?' Adam was startled. 'You don't want to see mine?'

'Yes, I jolly well do.'

The whole thing was a like a dream – not the Frights kind at all, but a sudden door opening onto a secret something else. Was this what grownups did?

'All right, then. If you really want to.'

'Of course I want to, silly,'

Adam unbuttoned his shorts and stood there in his white summer Deimals, feeling extraordinarily foolish and excited.

Lucy put out her hand and ran it firmly around his bottom and then up between his legs to the front, which made him wriggle with horror and delight.

'Shall I take them off?' she said.

'No. We mustn't.'

'Mine off first, of course.'

And she pulled at the white flowers to show him her pale pink stomach and the little crease like the coombe at Badgeworthy Water, and she took his hand and made him touch it, and then she bent over and showed him her real bottom with the wrinkle in the middle like a pink limpet, and she told him to touch that too, which made him feel disgraceful and punishable to death, and he actually hurt with the stiffness.

'Now,' she said. 'Yours down now.'

And she pulled the elastic that the Healthy Doctor had so thoughtfully provided and revealed it like a little white clothes-peg, and took it and rubbed it so hard it made him shout.

'Wheeeow.'

'Not so loud, silly,' she said, giving it another little tug. 'They'll hear us.'

'I want to wee-wee. Badly.'

'Good,' she said. 'Do it. I'll watch.'

'No. That's dirty.'

'Do it, I say.'

And she seized hold of it again.

'I wawawawa . . . ' was all he could say.

And then she showed him how she wee-weed, and was even going to show him more, when the proceedings were interrupted by a call from the house.

'Cooee. Children. Lunchtime.'

Lucy gave Adam a rueful smile, wiped her bottom with a large leaf, pulled up her white flowers, straightened her frock and turned into an angel again. Adam stood there with his clothes-peg, stricken with extra guilt at the sound of the grownup world.

'Come on,' said Lucy. 'I'm ravenous,' a phrase she had borrowed from her mother, who liked her food.

She pulled up his pants, buttoned up his trousers, gave him a kiss, and led him back to the house, looking as though

Cutcombe cream wouldn't melt in her mouth.

Later, at the table, he discovered, however, that it did — as did the ham and new potatoes, the Summer Pudding and the Fool. But, for himself, he was too preoccupied with his thoughts, which included stolen glances at Lucy, to surrender himself to the feast. He sensed that he had been introduced to something mystifying, brilliant, dangerous, but now almost within his understanding. Was this why grownups kept children in nurseries? Were they somehow frightened that they weren't childish enough and that they should be kept on ice, not for the children's good but for the sake of their parents? The thought lay as heavy on his stomach as breakfast bacon. He needed time to digest.

'Eat up, Adam,' said the Granny. 'What ails the child? We won't allow you down again if you can't appreciate Cutcombe provender. Look at your Cousin Lucy. And Badger, good old Badger. You look positively seedy.'

Badger, who'd taken extra potatoes, took a swipe at someone under the table. Lucy, on her second helping of ham, gave Adam a wink.

'These beans are stringy,' she said.

Adam could not imagine anything more audacious.

'Glad to see you two boys are getting on so well,' said the Granny to Rufus, who was nursing his knee. 'And what did you and Lucy get up to?'

'What do boys and girls usually get up to?' asked Chell, so quietly nobody heard her except Adam, who knew that somehow she must have spied on them.

'Adam showed me some botany, Great-Aunt,' said Lucy, straight-faced.

'Didn't know he knew any,' sniffed the Granny. 'You must've been a good influence on him, Lucy. You can have an extra chocolate afterwards.'

And afterwards, in the library, when the tin of chocolates was taken down from the highest shelf, Lucy did indeed get an extra dip into the treasure.

Sweets were so obviously the best things in the world that Adam once again spared a moment to ponder why grownups didn't spend their time devouring them. Why did they hold back? They had the reach, the freedom, the pocket-money.

Up till now, the mystery had been impenetrable, but, after his experiences among the laurels, he was beginning to wonder whether there might not be other sweets, more dangerous, more disturbing.

He chewed his piece of Hershey Bar (courtesy of Major Chuck), and looked across at Lucy, thoughtfully. Suddenly it didn't taste quite so good any more.

How could she look so angel-like after what had happened? It had happened, hadn't it? Or was it all sun and laurel fumes? (Rufus had said eating laurels could drive you mad, and he'd told him a story of how someone or other was killed by vapour just crossing a field on a hot day; not, admittedly, a laurel field, but it showed what fumes could do.)

He peered at Lucy again, but she wasn't giving anything away. Not even a bite of her extra piece of chocolate.

11

Franco, belying his customary air of debonair brutishness, was worried.

In terms of human relationship, he rated only one person as highly as his art, and that was his mother. He knew it was absurdly Italian of him but there it was. It is not easy to shake off the habits of a civilization.

His mother had, since 1937, been under threat from the Fascists. She herself did not know that she was in danger.

They had simply told her son that he might be able to be useful to them, and had he ever thought of working in England?

He had been obliged to concede that, yes, in spite of its food and its climate and the visual illiteracy of the populace, it might be a possible place to do a little sketching. And he learned that what they wanted was another agent, an agent with education and intelligence and a cast-iron excuse for moving around the countryside.

When war threatened, after he had satisfactorily passed back several juicy snippets about troop movements and armament depots, he had simply put a carefully drawn-up plan into operation. He had known that he was quite likely to be interned. He had also known that, once his usefulness was at an end, they could easily dispose of his mother, who had, to his dismay, now moved back to her home town in Germany. So he had married his English mistress, whom he found mildly amusing, which was really all one could expect of an English mistress, and he had moved down with her to West Somerset, where he could combine a little mild espionage with what turned out to be some really rather serious painting.

All had gone well at first. He had taken delivery of a transmitter which he had hidden in a disused quarry shaft frequented only by rats, bats and the occasional arthropod and concealed by dense undergrowth halfway up Cutcombe Hill.

He had thereupon scared off the two little boys of the house with a lively tale of bogies, and set himself to collect harmless morsels of local information which he could transmit every Saturday to his contact in France.

He wished them to be harmless because he was by no means a dedicated spy. He found the Nazis uncouth and churlish, and he had come to have an amused affection for the English, so he did his best to communicate items that, though they might seem useful, could be of no great consequence to anyone.

He did not, however, give it too much thought. He deemed himself to be above normal considerations of loyalty to his hosts. He was an artist. That was enough. The world must expect no more of him than to paint. These little snippets of his about Home Guard exercises and Land Army girls (some of whom he had found to have pretty little secrets of their own tucked under their breeches) were too absurd to take seriously when there was so much work to be done.

Just recently, though, as the tide of war had swung imperceptibly in favour of the Allies, he had noticed an increasing peremptoriness of tone creeping into his dialogue with Dürer (the name he had selected for his contact in France). There had been messages like 'Explain silence' and 'Send more gouache' (a reference to news of a more specifically military nature). Now, it seemed, they were particularly interested in any information relating to invasion plans for Northern France.

As he had sat in the damp cavern under Cutcombe Hill reflecting upon the unwelcome tenor of these recent communiqués, his fingers would automatically reach for the keyboard and begin to tickle out their own latest offering.

Bleep bleepbleep . . . blippety bleep . . .

'Cadet battalion, Taunton school, seen at Battle Camp near Dunster August 8th . . . '

But even as he did so, he knew that it was useless, and the inevitable reprimand would come winging through the ether as soon as he had finished sending.

Imbecile Goths. Why couldn't they leave him alone? What harm had his mother done to them − or anyone for that matter − beyond saving up her pitiful income (her husband, a minor bank official, had deserted her to live with a fifth rate chorus-girl from a provincial opera house) in order to send her son, after his spell in the Seminary, to a first-class art college? It might be an offence against art — certain critics had indeed suggested this might be the case — but then, with their record of aesthetic appreciation, you'd think the Nazis would find that no cause for displeasure.

No, reason and justice had nothing to do with it. They were barbarian blackmailers who wouldn't hesitate to dispose of an old woman if it suited their purpose. So he was going to have to sniff around for a nice juicy bone to placate them.

The obvious, though risky, place, of course, was the American base down at St Paget's Bay (which as well as gunnery training, sometimes served as a Transit Camp) — or the docks next door at Watchet. Here he might find the sort of information which would put him in the clear for many weeks.

So he had wheeled out his bicycle, loaded it up with a convincing cargo of artist's impedimenta, collected a couple of sandwiches and an admonition not to be home late because of the party at the Base that evening, and set off looking like a cross between the frontispiece for Trilby and an advertisement for Winsor & Newton.

On the way down the river, he had passed a parked jeep which he supposed belonged to the love-struck American (no doubt moping about the grounds). And this impression was confirmed when now, after twenty minutes' pedalling, he was almost at the gates of the Camp itself, and the Lieutenant suddenly appeared beside him in a cloud of pinkish Somerset dust.

Franco's brow darkened. He did not like feeling spied on.

'Hi,' said Thomas.

'Ho,' said Franco.

'It's off to work you go,' said Thomas.

'Just a little daubing,' explained Franco, English style. 'I am stufato with the woods and the hills and the kitchen garden and the Ferdy Fowler and even la bella Signora

Sanderson . . . ' He paused, giving Thomas a meaning look.

Thomas blushed suitably.

'And so I am off on my fiery-footed steed in search of pastures new.'

'Popular cities please us then, and the busy hum of men.'

'Exactly. Who say this busy ham?'

'Milton. Pastures new and all that.'

'He say that too. You surprise me, Thomaso. I thought Milton was disinfectant.'

Franco enjoyed teasing Thomas, but today, for some reason, Thomas wasn't having any.

'So you decided to come to the Base?'

'I came past the Base for the busy ham.' Franco suddenly sensed danger. 'I came past the Base on my way to wonderful Williton for the lively prosciutto.'

'And then?'

Really, thought Franco, this young man is becoming much too inquisitive. But, even as they talked, he peered past the jeep into the compound − and what he saw, though glimpsed fleetingly, tended to answer one of the questions Dürer had put to him. A truck with Canadian Army markings had driven past. He thought quickly, deciding to play the part of the insulted artist.

'It is plain, my dear Lippincott, that you are a man of limited sensitivity. You ask me "And then?" in that piscatorial voice, and I say to you, I do not know. Maybe I see something I like. Maybe not. I cannot tell you. I cannot tell myself. Maybe I go on to the sea.'

'To the docks?'

'To the sea, Mr Lippincott. What is the matter with you today?'

'I'm sorry. It's just . . . there may have been some kind of a leak.'

'Some kind of a leak? And you thought, I see it now, you thought I was a natural candidate for this trickling?'

'No . . . really . . . '

'Because I am an Italian. That is it, is it not? That is my crime. The crime of Leonardo and Michelangelo and the Brunelleschi and . . . Franco could feel his palms sweating. ' . . . Really, Mr Lippincott. Do I look like some kind of rusty bucket?'

'No, no, of course not. Just let us know if you see anything suspicious. Right? I have to go now. Sorry.'

Thomas was already beginning to feel ashamed of himself. He had a natural respect for the artist, and Franco's spirited counter-attack seemed to make particularly good sense. One could not condemn a guy for being Dante's fellow countryman. Besides, even if Franco were the spy, could he blame him? His own perceptions of right and wrong, negative and positive, were turning increasingly cloudy. Was this the beginning of schizophrenia? Or was the fission universal?

Franco watched as the Lieutenant drove in through the Base gate, half hating him for making his pulse race, and half sorry for him for being in love with that cow.

When the jeep was quite out of sight, he remounted and pedalled innocuously on towards Watchet, where, with some ingenuity and a considerable amount of luck, he was able to spot something which assured him beyond doubt that something very big indeed was going on, something that when he reported it that night would convince the sceptical Dürer that he was still indispensable.

What he had glimpsed, through the chink of an old lady's absent sailor-son's bedroom window (he had insinuated himself into her good graces by offering to paint the view as a present for her boy), was a cluster of landing-craft and what looked very much like an amphibious tank being loaded onto a converted ferry.

It wasn't so much a bone for the attentive watchdog in France. It was a whole fat juicy osso buco.

He would have a further look around at the Base party

this evening (it would be an easy matter to slip away from the lumpish scenes of Anglo-Saxon revelry). He would deliver his first draft later this afternoon, hot and strong, via his own secret service-lift up at the quarry-head. And he would follow it up with a full report tonight.

12

Upon the grassy slopes of an ancient mine-working on the western flank of Cutcombe Hill, Thomas and Julia had spread their picnic tea.

He had bought it from Williton because they guessed it might be imprudent to alert the Cutcombe kitchen to the assignation, but (with the aid of a Camel here and a Hershey bar there) it was the best tea that Williton could provide. There were cucumber sandwiches and little sweet tomatoes and home-made scones and clotted cream. But somehow neither of them was hungry.

They sat and held hands and sipped the Thermos-tasting tea, and listened to the distant guns on the range.

'Like a noise in dreams,' she said, surprisingly, reminding him of the morning, and of something else he'd done earlier.

After forking out forty Philip Morris for the cream, he'd paid a visit to the Williton Library where, some days earlier, he'd come across an unlikely copy of Jung's '*Synchronicity*', published in the States, sandwiched between the works of Captain W.E. Johns and Junior Red Cross Nurse. He had gone in again to memorize a passage that seemed both troubling and important.

'Experiments show that, in relation to the psyche, space and time are so-to-speak elastic and can apparently be reduced to vanishing-point, as though they were dependent on psychic conditions and did not exist in themselves, but were merely suggested by the conscious mind', he had read, with the scones pressed hot against his shirt.

It expressed something of what he'd been feeling, and now he told her about it.

'Explain.'

'I can't really. It's as though Time had walls which might actually melt if the conditions were right, so you could go through.'

'And what does that mean?'

'I don't know. Don't you feel, though, sometimes, that things aren't quite what they seem?' he gestured vaguely.

'Like?'

'It's as though it's all not really here. Like, yes, like a noise in dreams . . . Don't laugh,' he said, 'but I think it's going on right now. Oh, I know it's a bee in my particular bonnet, but I keep getting the feeling that . . . Time's not very stable around here . . . '

'Stable?'

'Theoretically,' said Thomas, warming to his bee, 'that would be associated with some kind of electro-magnetic disturbance. But we've had nothing round here more electrically disturbed than Chell's hearing-aid . . . '

'But wouldn't more people know about this Time thing? I mean, it can't happen a lot . . . there'd be letters to *The . . . Times . . . *'

'It may be happening a hell of a lot, but we're simply not aware of it. Like a projector, the light, our awareness, shines through just one aperture.'

'So how do *you* know about it?'

'I don't know. I just sense it. Maybe that's how I got interested in the first place. Some people have second sight. Maybe I've got Time-sight. Or maybe I've just got an overactive imagination.'

She leant over and kissed him on the mouth.

'I'm here,' she said, 'I'm real.'

'It's just . . . I'm afraid of losing you,' he said, 'I'm afraid it'll all be wiped out, that you'll go back to being a stranger. Or vanish altogether down the wainscoting.'

They were silent for a few moments.

'You like to quote,' she said, changing the subject, a moth of disquiet fluttering about her mind.

'I know,' he said. 'It's a bad habit.'

'It's not that, at least not when you do it,' she told him. 'But I hate it when people use other people's lines to show how awfully sensitive they are. Like people who endlessly tell funny stories to show their wit.'

'I think it's because I sometimes haven't got the courage to say things in my own words. And sometimes I haven't got the words to say things in my own wit.'

'Men were always writing me poems when I was young. I usually found out later that they came from the *Golden Treasury*. It was like being kissed by a ghost.'

'It's strange,' he said, 'I'd never have thought you'd say that kind of thing. You're full of surprises.'

'I'm a looking-glass person. I'm what's expected of me by whoever I'm with. That's why I'm not very good for you, I'm afraid.'

'I don't think you believe that.'

'No, listen, Thomas. You have to try and understand.'

She had never been so honest with herself before — let alone with anybody else — which was why she was in such a danger of falling in love with him. He improved her value. She felt like a park after a visit from Capability Brown.

It was funny how, in a way he reminded her of Tristram in the early days. As if Tristram were a rehearsal for the real thing. But whereas he was held back in a cat's cradle of Cutcombery, always conscious of position, always concerned not just with *doing* but with *being* the Right Thing, Thomas was somehow both hurtable and totally open. It was his great strength.

'I know you're there inside,' he was saying, 'you've just been waiting for the right moment to come out. Really,' he said, 'I'm just a sort of fumbling Aladdin. You're the genie.'

'And what is your wish, Master?' she said, genially.

'I'm so happy, it's pathetic,' he said.

She did not tell him that she knew herself too well and that, though she might respond to a Capability Brown, her nature would quickly reassert itself, brambles of laziness, convolvuli of listlessness, that fatal weakness of hers, which over and over again had obscured the broad avenue and elmy vistas that life had put at her disposal.

She didn't tell him because half of her wanted to believe in her transformation as much as he did. She could see herself as gracious, civilized, kind and patient, with an adoring husband and seraphic children; but on the other hand, she would visualize a creature vacillating, neglectful, wilful and destructive.

> Can a mother's tender care
> Cease toward the child she bare?
> Yes, she may forgetful be . . .

Indeed, she was forgetful, an unsatisfactory mother and a faithless wife, but self-realization was a far cry from self-correction.

'Look, wild strawberries,' she said, 'let's pick some. You've brought such a beautiful tea, and all I want's wild strawberries. Forgive me?'

'Sure,' he said. 'I don't know that I've ever tasted them.'

'They're gorgeous,' she said, 'my mother-in-law grows them in her rock-garden, but she's the only one who's ever allowed to eat them. She devours them with a ghastly pippy noise at breakfast.'

Relieved at the prospect of action, which consequently would exempt her from speaking about her feelings —

which, if it hadn't already been a difficult area for her, was much discouraged by Cutcombe society, and therefore in a state of some atrophy among all natives — Julia became more cheerful.

'See who can pick most in twenty minutes,' she said. 'Bet I can beat you.'

'What's the prize?' he asked, relieved, in his turn, by any action that might delay the eventual outcome — the dreaded finding-out of whether she really meant what she had promised him, and if (such was the state of his nervous anticipation) he were capable of tasting love's thrice-repured nectar.

'The loser pays a forfeit,' she said.

The wild strawberry, normally a shy plant, had become positively forward on the crumbled slate of the Old Quarry. The only problem for the gatherer was that other flora had become equally exuberant. Stonecrop and wallpepper, pimpernel and willowherb, foxglove and pellitory rioted nimbly of the sapling-fringed plateaux of slag, while further into the hillside, rowan and ash, ivy and bramble, sallow, elder and old man's beard pried into the roofless mine-buildings, licked into the shafts, frolicked across the old mineral line and squeezed once-broad pathways into mere indentations of foliage.

They spread out the napkins he had brought, and started to pick, knee by knee, on the more accessible banks which skirted the clearing where they had been sitting.

Far below, as they gathered, they could see a pennant of smoke as the beetle-crusher wound its way along the shore-track from Dunster to Minehead.

'Is that why it's called Minehead? Because of the mines?' Thomas asked.

'I don't think so,' said Julia, 'Minehead's a corruption of Mohun's Hyde. The Mohuns were the family who ran this part of the world under the Conqueror, and a hyde was

161

simply a measure of land. At least that's what the Reverend Biddle told me with his hand rather too emphatically on my knee.'

'Then it must be true,' said Thomas.

'You mustn't talk,' she said. 'You've got to concentrate. Otherwise you may lose.'

She moved over the ridge of one of the quarry's undulating barrow-like protuberances, and gradually disappeared from sight, gleaming brown hair hiding her face as she bent earnestly over the matter in hand, brown legs neatly tucked up among the unimaginable privileges of the recesses of her lime-green frock.

Thomas reflected for a moment on the incredible antiquity of the country, so different from his own, and marvelled at the way the British could just throw off a fact like that − Mohun's Hyde − as if it were no more than a bookish appendix, fit only for fusty pedagogues; sort of there, don't you know, but bad form to talk about too much.

Mohun's Hyde. How he loved this place. It was partly, of course, that she was English, and he loved it for her sake, but it was more than that. The towns, the villages, the very names of the woods and hills filled him with a sense of magic and a kind of prospectorly lust, as though history were an energy which the land contained like coal.

He shook himself slightly. This was no moment for reverie. She had more or less promised him the prize. All he had to do was gather.

He now turned his attention to a rich seam of little suckers which ran towards the upper end of the quarry along the remains of one section of line. Broken remnants of wagon and old shards of machinery shared the afternoon sunlight with a variety of bindweeds and honeysuckles beside a shattered engine house.

In spite of the afternoon's heat, Thomas felt a tremor of apprehension; there was an eeriness about the place which he found hard to define. He put it down to the industrial nature of the ruins. They seemed somehow much more derelict, more defeated than if they had simply been cottages or a chapel, but he wondered vaguely whether the place were haunted, whether perhaps some accident had taken place there, a cave-in maybe, a berserk beam-engine. No wonder that kid Adam thought the Frights lived up here.

He peered in at one of the windows, and there was a nasty scuffling in the darkness which made him peer quickly out again. Now, of all times, he didn't want to think of darkness.

He shook himself now, reminding himself he was a Lieutenant and a big boy now, and anyway he was wasting too much time in speculation when there were more pressing matters in hand.

He glanced at his watch. There was still ten minutes to go. Where had those goddam strawberries got to?

Behind the engine house there was a small clearing which looked promising from a distance but, on closer inspection, turned out to be void. A rich haul of ragged robin, but that wasn't going to bring home the bacon. Eight minutes left.

Just at this moment, when panic was beginning to press the red button somewhere behind his left temple and the old sensations of being confronted with an impossible equation throughout the duration of an entire exam came back to make his palms prickle, he spotted a small track leading into what seemed to be the very side of the hill, with a whole convoy of little green plants suffused with red berries straggled up each side as if surprised by Stukas.

Stooping energetically, he began to gather them with a will. Then he noticed two things.

The track had been recently used. There were boot marks in the boggy places where a small stream wriggled through. And a small artist's watercolour brush was lying in the grass at his feet.

Laying his cargo of fruit carefully on the ground, he cautiously moved forward down the pathway. A pheasant started noisily from a bush over to his right, making him jump like a wildebeeste, but he recovered his composure and pressed on.

Turning a corner, he was finally confronted by a mass of convolvulus and ivy that appeared to bar the way, and he was about to turn back, irritated with himself for having wasted precious minutes from his assignment, when something made him give the tangle of vegetation a pummel. It moved back, over-easily.

He took one end of the general matting, and folded it back. Darkness seemed to well out of the hillside, but eventually a little daylight gained admission, allowing him to discern a partially caved-in tunnel furnished near the mouth with some ammunition boxes, a canvas chair and a folding camp-table. This was no doubt the place that the kid Adam had been warned off. The Frights were a scaring device.

Cautiously, in case there were someone lurking in the shadows, he moved forward.

Base Intelligence Officer he might be, but he was not trained in the due procedures of military forensics. What did one do with one's footprints? Should one be wearing finger-stalls? Was one, in fact, catching a spy at all or was one trespassing on an artist's withdrawing room? The only artist he knew around here was not the sort of artist one would like to brush with.

How difficult it all was — especially with the pressing engagement waiting for him on the hill of summer. A sudden shaft of unrealizable longing shot through him for the hectic unimportances of university life, the life he had enjoyed before his fall from grace. But there was no profit in that kind of thinking. He was too far in, in every way, for that. The past was a sealed unit. He slipped one of his pills in his mouth. They sometimes helped when things got fraught.

He advanced upon the packing-cases and removed a lid. What he saw — a dull metallic box equipped with knobs, dials and a set of headphones — convinced him that he had indeed stumbled upon the unmistakable appurtenances of espionage.

He felt in turn exhilaration, vexation, sorrow and dismay.

There was the natural elation of the chase, like starting a hare or finding a mushroom, and the sense that, with his discovery (although inadvertent), he had proved himself the equal if not the superior of Major Chuck. There was annoyance because he still had unfinished business with Julia, who with her strawberry hoard must now look like one of those allegorical figures so admired by the Late Renaissance. And then there was regret — because however he might deplore the giving away of Allied military secrets and the arrant betrayal of trust that Franco had perpetrated, he still admired the artist and respected the man.

Somewhere behind, he heard Julia calling him. Hastily obliterating any traces of his visit, which really meant feeling foolish and scuffing vaguely at the dusty floor, he pulled the curtain of undergrowth down across the entrance again, picked up his lamentably inadequate cargo of fruit and walked back to the clearing, where he found her lying in the sun with a leaf over each eye.

'Where have you *been*? I was *lonely* ,' she said, stressing the words in mock-petulance.

He knelt down beside her, his heart beating like a snared badger, and removed the leaves with his lips, noticing as he did so that her collection of berries had by no means come up to the profusion of his imaginings. It was clearly forfeit time.

But first he kissed her eyelids flutteringly with his own.

'Chinese?' she asked, 'or is it Eskimo?'

'Yes,' he said, pushing a wild strawberry like an amorous jujube through her quarter-open lips.

'Mmm,' she said, 'that's gorgeous. Who won?'

'I did. Though I'm too much of a gentleman to say so.'

'I wasn't really trying.'

'Sour grapes.'

'Sweet grapes,' she said as he pushed another berry through the gates.

'Anyway,' he said, 'you strained every sinew.'

'I didn't,' she said. 'Fell. Feel my sinews.'

She extended a languid leg towards him, revealing a milk-and-honey land of thigh. He felt her sinews.

'See. They're limp as anything. No strain.'

They were a great deal limper than his procreative member, which was surging about in his trousers like a rogue torpedo.

'Oh golly,' he said, all thought of the cache in the tunnel being firmly relegated to bottom of the league.

'You mustn't fall in love with me,' she said. 'Darling Capability Thomas.'

'It's not me I'm worried about,' he said. 'I think it's you. I don't think it's ever happened to you before.'

She sat up and looked at him unblinkingly for a few moments. Then she dipped a white and red strawberry in the carton from Williton, and ate it pensively, grimacing a little at the sharpness before it was allayed by the cream. Like her, she thought, a little spurt of keen intent, and then a drift into the easy way.

And then again, she thought, no, there is a chance here. He's kind and intelligent and maybe there is a start again in America. Maybe I can leave all this behind and take the boys (I suppose I should take the boys?) and get out of that dreadful house. At least, I could if there wasn't a war on. Or perhaps we could anyway, brave the convoys, sail over and wait for him. But what if he goes and gets himself killed? What then?

So many maybes, so many risks. Too many. I really can't cope with all those decisions. There must be some way I can make him see. But not now.

Somewhere, high above, a skylark was singing. Thomas reached over and picked a dog-rose, put it in her hair, knelt down and kissed her dress delicately above the left nipple.

'Forfeit,' he said.

The sunshine burned and burrowed between her legs where the frock had ridden up. She made no attempt to redress the matter.

'Let's take our clothes off,' she said.

Thomas was momentarily startled.

This was not quite as he had imagined it, but nothing seemed quite to be working out according to the rules of the courtly norm. One doesn't reckon on unearthing enemy agents while trysting one's true-love, or, if one does, one looks for it in vain in the Oxford Book of Ballads. Mind you, there might be some interesting parallels in the Morte d'Arthur. Medieval precedent or not, however, it would justify his absence, to say nothing of the use of the jeep, to Major Chuck – and two birds with one stone was a sentiment which Sir Gawain himself would, in similar circumstances, have condoned.

As a matter of fact, Julia had surprised herself. It was just that she had suddenly had a vision of them dancing naked, immemorially, round and round in a ring, while mysterious birds indicative of this and that piped in the shadows and an ape threw fruit from a baobab tree.

Unbuttoning her frock, she stepped out of it with such a delightful grace that Thomas nearly swooned.

'I die, I faint, I fail . . . '

She was wearing hardly anything underneath, and her skin had a hue that made Cutcombe cream look muddy. However beautiful she might look dressed, he thought, he would always resent her clothes as being mere impedimenta to her greater beauty.

His hands, without knowing what they did, scrabbled at his shoes and shirt.

She undid her brassiere, revealing breasts of extraordinary roundness and firmness, with nipples ruddier than the wild strawberry and fifty times as delicious.

He stood before her naked, feeling the sun on places where the sun had never shone.

'I feel the sun on places where the sun has never shone.'

'Socks, Thomas.'

He didn't even feel foolish. Her nipples were simply asking for teaspoons and sugar, and he had to restrain himself from pressing on each one a tiny dollop from the Williton carton.

She took off her pants, revealing the slenderest isosceles of dark brown curls, and held out her arms to him.

There was a hush in the glade. A red squirrel, fooling about in a mountain-ash, paused and peered, wrinkling its nose and twiddling its thumbs. If reedy pipes had started to play, and a grinning face with horns and parted the sallows, they wouldn't have been in the least surprised. It was one of those moments of pure magic that go on hanging in the memory like a starburst long after the minor squibs and candles have faded into night.

They stood and kissed and felt each other's warmth. And then, without speaking, they lay down. And Thomas (who had some experience of near-impotence at similar testing moments, finding that the sudden proximity of naked strangers made him nervous rather than priapic) all at once discovered he was very deeply inside her without even knowing quite how he got there. It seemed to him to be the very best thing that had ever happened. The warmth, the fragrance, the terrible tenderness, the awareness of the explosive cargo of nitroglycerine in his loins, all made him want to stop, it was so dangerous to go on.

'I want to stay like this, Siamesely like this, always,' he said.

Her previous experiences had been mere couplings.

'It's the first time,' she said, 'Siamesely, always . . .'

His hands were doing things that others had done before, but whereas previously it had given her power, it now drew from her a delicious panic. We can't. Stop. She could feel herself, luscious and open, wonderfully open, like a paw-paw.

'There,' she said, 'your hand . . . there . . . wonderful . . .'

Darling, we can't, it won't work, oh yes. Yes. Now now. This was it. Now. The first time. Circles and circles, wider and wider, Excalibur in the lake.

And then, too, like the massed choirs of San Marco bursting into a Cavalli Gloria, like the explosion of light in the Giorgione Revelation, like a Gatling-gun in old Mrs Sanderson's greenhouse, Thomas did it as well.

And Chelly-Chops, who had followed Julia up the path as she had slipped out during siesta time, Chelly-Chops who never slept, hard-bitten guardian of all that was seen and had yet to be told, bitter hermit of the wavelengths, even Chelly-Chops turned away feeling a little bit ashamed of herself, and wandered back along the path by the stream, reflecting that whatever advantage her secrets would bring her, whatever hold she might win over however many people (and it didn't look like being many), she would never experience the rapture of idyllic copulation which — more than the fruits of genius or the comforts of philosophy or the afterglow of charity or the contemplation of the navel — is the nearest humanity ever gets to the condition of the gods.

'Darling?'

Julia spoke after a long interval.

'Yes?'

'You won't fall in love with me?'

'Why not?'

'I have. With you.'

'Then why shouldn't I? It doesn't seem fair.'

'Because I know.'

'Not that again.'

'Because I'm married. Because I can't cope with obstacles. Because you're young and poor. Because I'm older than you are. Because there's a war on.'

'Because,' he said scornfully, 'of nothing. All nothing.'

'Because of chalk and cheese. Of ships and sealing wax.'

'Don't worry,' he said. 'That's the important thing. There's plenty of time. We'll talk about it later. It's all going to be all right.'

'It must be the up after the down,' he told himself. 'I'm the last person to be relentlessly cheerful. But it can't go wrong now, it simply can't.'

'Boboom. Bobooom. Boomboomboomboom.

The guns were firing in the Channel again.

> For Fate with jealous eye doth see
> Two perfect loves, nor lets them close,
> Their junction would her ruin be,
> And her tyrannic power depose.

He looked at his watch. It was after five. He had promised Major Chuck he would be back at the Base at half-past four.

'God,' he said, 'I have to move now. There's things I have to do for the party. You are coming, aren't you? Aren't you?'

'I shall dress to kill,' she said.

'Haven't you done enough already?'

'I am insatiable. I have a lust for blood.'

She bared her teeth dracularly.

'I'm feeling in the jugular vein myself.'

He swooped on her and gently bit her neck, then straightened his tie, put on his cap and picked up the barely broached picnic.

'I really have to go now. See you around eight at the bar. I love you,' he said.

She watched him as he ran down the track towards the

little lane where he'd parked his jeep, the sun still high enough over Cutcombe Hill to make his shadow the same length as his body. It was a magical moment. Thomas had told her the ancient Celts had a word for it. If you caught a man asleep at that precise moment, you could steal his shadow and do what you liked with him.

'Look after your shadow,' she called. 'It's thingummy hour.'

He waved, clasping himself.

She very much hoped he was going to be all right.

13

Tristram woke up in a woodcutter's shed among fir trees, and peered at the sky. It seemed to be late afternoon. He did not know where he was or how he had got there, but he sensed that he was nearing his destination.

Now he thought about it, he remembered rushing head-long through a thicket of young saplings that smacked at his face as he fought to reach the bottom of a narrow valley. The dogs were after him. Poor Tom will throw his head at them.

It came back to him now. In the half-dark of dawn he had come sliding down a wooded hillside straight into a farm-yard, and all the hounds of Hell seemed to have been alerted. Mercifully most of them were chained, but a small collie-like sheepdog leapt assiduously after him as faces appeared at the corners of blacked-out windows.

He could not help feeling, even in his fear and exhaustion, that his retreat lacked something of dignity. If one was going to die, one should do so with fixed bayonet and face to the enemy, not scampering wildly into a gully with

171

one's pants worried by mongrels.

Floundering into the stream, it was wide and shallow and pebbly, he splashed along its course for several minutes, noting with relief that the dog had ceased its pursuit and was yapping futilely some way back along the bank.

He had rounded a curve in the valley. The first bird's-egg blue of morning was beginning to insinuate itself among a speckle of stars. He couldn't remember having eaten for days, but now, more than anything else, he wanted to sleep, so he left the river and plunged into the forest — familiar densely-packed conifers clinging to the slopes of his childhood — Brittany, of course, just across the water. It was strange how his concentration seemed to come and go. Au joli bois je m'en vais.

What had Ferdy Fowler been doing there anyway? And Marmaduke? Surely he had no part in this. One wouldn't require a goose on such an important mission.

And why had it said Hollcombe Water Farm at that place with the dogs? This was scarcely Breton? Or had it all been long ago riding with the foxhounds?

There was no doubt that time had been playing tricks with him, and now, though he felt better after his sleep, his attention still kept wandering and it seemed to him that his situation, whatever it was, could only be glimpsed fitfully as it were through storm-driven clouds.

He knew that something had to be done, and he indeed seemed impelled in the general direction of where it should take place, but he couldn't say what or where it might be. He simply knew he had to get there and do it. Soon.

But if they would let him stop and think for a bit, they might get a damn sight better job out of him. If only they would turn that light out.

Light. Electricity. That was it. The man with the transmitter, the message back to base. His call-sign, what was it?, Sugar Uncle Lima Lima Yolk. Sully. Little sop to the Free French, Sunray Major had said. Whoever Sully was.

172

'Are you receiving me?'

'Loud and confused, Sunray. Through clouds.'

'I say again . . . '

'Hullo, Squarey. What are you doing here? Decent of you to come along. We'll go up to Our Place again. Remember? No grownups . . . '

They had held each other's tools there, when Squarey had come to stay in the school holidays, and then at the beginning of the next term he had let Squarey down and gone to share a study with Bradbrook.

'I was sorry about that, Squarey. Caddish of me. Come along. I'll show you the way.'

He wished Squarey would keep still. And why was it he appeared to be still only thirteen?

'Bet you've been in a space rocket at the speed of light, Squarey. Is that what it is?'

But Squarey had disappeared as suddenly as he had come.

A couple of rabbits were hobnobbing confidentially just in front of the hut. Far away there was the sound of gunfire, but it didn't seem to disturb them.

Jerry guns. The ones he was going to help to silence.

He rather envied the rabbits but decided that they might have guns on their minds as well; they just didn't believe in unnecessary demonstration; funny thing for French rabbits.

Thinking of French rabbits made him think of French letters — so embarrassing to buy — remember forming up at that little health and efficiency shop behind the Cornmarket with Bradbrook — and even more embarrassing to use — which made him think of Griselda though she'd hardly be flattered to hear it — and how he'd made such an ass of himself when they'd spent that night in London — and of how little he knew her and how much he wanted to discover more — unlike his wife, whom he hardly knew from the start and every time they met he felt he knew a little less — like Space really, there'd been a craze for it at school, as well as French letters — stars coming towards you and stars retreating — Griselda was a blue shift, his wife was red — and the boys, little Hottentots, homunculi whose only connection with him was that some necessary electric part of their starter-button had been housed in his testicles, a shaft of light from his penis into the swirling matrix of the mother — and speaking of mothers, what about his own — had he ever really found shelter in that horrid, in that horrid cave? Horribile dictu. It must be so — though now he felt the impossibility of the connection. It had really been better with Squarey, but he loved Zelda more, even though no doubt he'd let the side down next time . . .

More sleep. That was the thing, and then the last bit in the dark. After that, they could do what they liked with him. It would be a relief to get it all over.

14

Nanny had bicycled over to see old Mrs Nethercott at Luxborough, who was a witch, and reputed to be cunning about women's problems.

Mrs Nethercott's cottage smelt of ancient hams, paraffin, cats and Mrs Nethercott, and Nanny entered with mingled distaste, misgiving and confusion. She was, after all, the miller's daughter, which mean she was above the common villagers' superstitions. But she needed help beyond the capacity of her father's whirling machinery.

'Sit 'ee down, m'dear.'

Nanny sat on the edge of a high-backed settle beside the fire, and next to a large corn-dolly. She hoped there wouldn't be any creepy-crawlies coming out of it.

'Don't be afeard, m'dear. Now do 'ee tell us all about ut.'

'I think I'm . . . going to have a baby, Mrs Nethercott.'

''Es that all? Come, m'dear. 'Ee've got nothin' to worrit about. Lot of wimmen come to Oi 'cos they cain't. If 'ee'd come to Oi and said, "Mrs Nethercott, Oi want babbies", now Oi moight ev to put on moi thinkun-cap. Do 'ee 'ave the babby and enjoy ut.'

'Yes, but you see, Mrs Nethercott, I'm not married.'

'Ar.'

Mrs Nethercott poked the fire and mumbled a little to herself. Then she looked very directly at Nanny with eyes strangely brilliant in the old chamois-leather of her face.

''Ave 'ee got summat with 'ee?'

'Summat? I mean, something?'

'Aye. Summat.'

'Nothing . . . Apart from what I come to get rid of.'

Nanny felt herself lapsing into the dialect of her childhood. She didn't know what Nanny over at Combe Huish would say, but then Nanny at Combe Huish wasn't pregnant, or if she was it'd be a bloody miracle seeing as she was past fifty-five.

'There's summat around 'ee. Carnt say what ut is. Not your fault, mind, not saying ut's essackly your fault, but there's summat there and ut's not very noice. You been mixing with funny folk? Casting spells and such?'

'No . . . No.'

'The big house. That's where it come from . . . '

Nanny pulled herself together. She hadn't come for spooky talk.

'What about my problem, Mrs Nethercott?'

The old woman seemed put out.

'Don't 'ee interrupt, m'dear. Us'll come to your babby all in good time. What Oi wants to know is . . . what's going on up there?'

'There's no casting spells that's for certain. Unless it's

175

young Mrs Sanderson making eyes at them Yanks. Or the old girl with the hearing aid popping up when you don't expect ut.'

'Noo . . . it's not thart. Any kiddies up thar? Little boys mebbe?'

'Of course. I mean, yes. That's why I'm there. Looking after un.'

'Well 'ee bain't looking arter un very well, m'dear. 'Ee wants to take more care of they. There's a load o' mischief over the 'ouse. Who's the fader?'

'He's away with the military.'

Mrs Nethercott cackled and prodded Nanny's midriff.

'Noo. Your spot of bother, m'dear. Who's the fader?'

'I can't tell 'ee.'

'Can't tell or don't know?'

'Can't tell,' said Nanny, indignantly.

'If 'ee don't tell us the fader, us can't do nuthin' for 'ee, m'dear.'

'Well . . . It's Rodgers. Rodgers the Cowman.'

Mrs Nethercott didn't seem in the least surprised. It even struck Nanny that she knew already. The sooner she got out of here the better, she thought, but she couldn't leave without getting what she came for.

'Ay . . . Johnny Rodgers. Rodgers by name and Rodgers by nature,' said Mrs Nethercott.

'Don't say that. Oi luv 'im.'

'Course you do, m'dear, course you do. But what do Missus Rodgers say about ut?'

'She don't know yet. 'E's going to tell 'er.'

Mrs Nethercott got up, creaky as a mill-cog, went over to an ancient cupboard, and extracted a small dark-brown vial which she pressed into Nanny's hand.

'Course 'e is, m'dear. On Judgement Day but not before. Now 'ee take the drops, three every night, two every morning, and let Nature take uts course. Thats be one guinea exackly, m'dear.'

Nanny was momentarily outraged.

'A guinea? But Oi only earns ten pound a week.'

''Eee won't be earning nuthin' at all if 'ee don't take un double quick.'

Nanny pocketed the vial, handed over the money and pedalled glumly back up the road the way she'd come.

'And 'ee mind the little boys, see,' shouted Mrs Nethercott, her whiskers glowing red in the late sunshine.

('Carn't 'ave a witch without whiskers,' she used to say to her cat Luttrell, who liked to pounce at them when he wasn't running errands. 'We'd 'ave the Beast o' Brendon comin' to pay us a visit to inspect our curdentials.')

She watched the departing figure with some satisfaction.

'Didn't know Missus Rodgers was called Nethercott before 'er got wed, did 'ee, m'dear?'

But Nanny was already out of earshot, and labouring her way up Luxborough Hill.

15

Cutcombe teatime, with its immemorial odour of methylated spirits burning like incense in the great silver lozenge under the hot water pot, sputtered along as dimly as the flame itself. It was not a successful meal as Cutcombe teas went. The cream had gone sour, Chell was late and the Mother had not turned up at all.

'Where is the girl?' the Granny remarked, testily.

No one knew.

'So inconsiderate,' said Granny — it was one of her favourite words — 'And where have you been, Chell? I don't ask much, but the least I expect is punctuality at mealtimes.'

'What?' said Chell. 'Oh, so sorry. Adding to my Collection. Didn't hear the stable clock.'

'Well, I'm glad to hear at least you were usefully employed.'

No one knew what Chell's Collection was, or even ever cared to ask. It was enough, however, for the Granny that she was Doing Something. Idleness was another of the great sins in the Cutcombe canon — even when Doing Something might be self-defeating, dangerous or aphasically boring.

The boys sat and ate their bread and butter before they could have some cake.

'What about you, Adam?' said the Granny, casting about for a scapegoat, 'what have you been up to?'

After Lucy and her family had left for home again, he had spent the afternoon thinking about her bottom, but he didn't think this would meet with quite the right measure of approval.

'I've been um painting,' he lied, adding unnecessarily, 'painting some pictures.'

Art was good but a lie was terrible, and Granny had a nose for unearthing mendacity that would have made her the cynosure of the interrogation rooms at Toledo. No need for the Rack and Iron Maiden when Granny was around.

'Ha,' she said, 'we have a budding Titian in our midst. After tea we must all have a look.'

Adam's heart plummeted. Why had he not thought of this obvious comeback? The only picture he had in his painting-book was one that the Granny had already criticized exhaustively. Would he have time to race up, paint three more, and then hurtle down again? He very much doubted it. Once again, he was going to be caught out in a lie — which according to Granny was yet another of the worst things you could possibly do — even worse than

178

burping in church. For himself, he thought looking at little girls' bottoms while they did wee-wee was probably worse still, but he didn't feel prepared to contest the issue with her. He would settle for her marking.

What he couldn't quite understand was why it was so bad for little boys to tell lies when grownups seemed to do it whenever they felt like it.

He looked at Rufus, expecting no assistance, and received none.

Gloomily munching seed-cake, having polished off the statutory two slices of Hovis, he was bracing himself for the inevitable discovery, humiliation and punishment, when help came from an unexpected quarter. Across the hall, in the library, the telephone started to ring.

'Who can that be?' said Granny. 'At teatime too. So inconsiderate.'

The telephone was answered. There was a pause. And then Amy, the parlour-maid, came in.

'It's for you, mum,' she said, 'it's a Colonel. I didn't catch his name.'

The Granny looked concerned.

'Oh dear,' she said, 'I hope it's not . . .'

As she rose and walked across to the hall, she rehearsed her family connections in case of bad news. There was her nephew James in Africa, and her Cousin Alice's boy in India, and . . .

When she returned her face was distemper-coloured.

'What is it?' said Chell encouraged into sharpness. 'Who is it now?'

Chell seemed to be growing in stature just as the Granny miraculously appeared to be shrivelling.

'It's . . . it's . . . pas devant les enfants . . .'

'Shoo,' said Chell to the boys, 'come along. Jump to it.'

'But . . .' said Rufus.

'I said "out",' said Chell.

The boys snatched what they could from their plates

179

and scuttled from the room.

'Well?' demanded Chell of the quivering matriarch. 'What is it?'

'It's . . . it's . . . Tristram . . . '

'Dead?' enquired Chell, tactlessly.

'No . . . no . . . worse . . . ' whispered the Granny.

'Raped?' thought Chell, with a still voice.

'The . . . my son . . . oh, this would break his father's heart . . . '

The Granny clutched at her bosom and it seemed quite possible that she might start tearing at her hair.

'But what's happened?' reiterated Chell.

'It was his Colonel calling. Apparently Tristram was on very special training for something the Colonel couldn't talk about on the telephone – you'd expect him to be chosen for that kind of task . . . '

'Yes?' said Chell, almost impatiently.

'And they were having this very exhaustive, well, battle-course dress-rehearsal to make sure he was the right man for the job, which of course he was . . . you know how exhaustive dress-rehearsals can be . . . I remember J.M. Barrie having one at the Haymarket that went on from five till . . . '

'Go on,' said Chell.

'They'd flown him down and dropped him over Dartmoor, Tristram I mean, not J.M. Barrie . . . and, right in the middle of an interrogation survival routine, whatever that may be, apparently Tristram very properly escaped, but then just . . . disappeared. The Colonel didn't like to use the word "deserted" but he used it all the same. It's just possible, he said, that he might be suffering from some sort of brainstorm, but I told him that was most unlikely . . . . Tristram was never weak. Nor was he, I told the Colonel, an arrant poltroon. But the man kept insisting he might turn up here, and I was to let him know as soon as he did. There must be some kind of explanation, Chell. I don't

180

know what to think. This is going to make worm's meat of me.'

She hid her face in her hands extravagantly, and Chell unleashed a small pinched smile of triumph.

16

Thomas drove home with a bravura performance on the gear-shift of the long-suffering Willys jeep, revving and double-declutching and making the precarious machine bound and jump like a dog that sees its master in high spirits.

He executed a pretty curvet as he drove in at the main gates, and his crest fell only marginally when the Duty Sergeant informed him that Major Caldwell wanted to see him an hour ago or sharper.

He parked the jeep and wandered over to the Major's room where he found him sitting on his bed struggling with a knotted festoon of fairy lights.

'Where the motherfuckin' hell have you been?' asked the Major.

'Good news, Major,' said Thomas, grinning all over his head.

'What the hell's that supposed to mean?'

'I got him.'

'What?'

'That's right. Kind of. I haven't got him but I've got him if you follow my drift.'

'Listen, Lippincott. You know what?'

'What?'

'If you had a bit more grip, you'd be a first-class asshole.'

'I wouldn't say that.'

'You don't have to say it, Lippincott. I say it. You say what I want you to say. Why do you think we're fighting this war, Lippincott?'

'Something about Freedom?'

'Precisely. Now . . . Freedom is in a hurry, Lippincott. Freedom is not going to sit around scratching its fanny waiting for you to make a sensible report. Freedom does not want a sonnet or an ottava rima or a perfumed essay, Lippincott, nor even, and this may come as a shock to you, a nine-volume excursion round your foreskin in rhymed hexameters. What Freedom wants, while guns roar, earth gapes, towns tumble and men roast in boiling oil on their way to the cold buffet in Davy Jones's finny self-serve, is brevity, accuracy, and despatch. Now shoot.'

Thomas was not a little impressed at the crude vigour and unexpected breadth of syllable in the Major's tirade (had he misjudged the man?), and hastily told him everything that had happened, only leaving out the fruits of his amatory experiences.

The Major, however, was not completely satisfied.

'How did you stumble across this place, Lippincott?'

'Intuition. Hunch. Flair. Deduction. Induction.'

'And seduction, Lippincott? The location you describe is, I note, in the purlieus of our good friend and neighbour at Cutcombe Hall. Did you not happen to see a certain lady in your travels?'

'Certainly not, Major. I am not to be deflected by a ripe lip and a soft cheek. I have had the Italian under observation for some time. I simply followed my nose and put two and two together.'

'As long as you didn't follow your cock, and put one and one together.'

'Really, Major, I don't think . . . '

He had not misjudged the man. He was beyond the pale.

'That's all right, Lippincott. You did well. What's the next move?'

182

'I suggest I keep him under constant observation, Major. He suspects nothing at the moment. We'd like to know who he's contacting, what he's transmitting. Right? In fact, until we do, we have no definite proof that he's actually in touch with anyone. He's coming to the party tonight. I'll watch him to see if he tries to snoop around.'

'And then tomorrow we'll tell the British and they can take care of the whole thing. Just as well we got rid of the goddam Canadians. That was Top Security.'

'They've moved on?'

'Yeah. Gone south. Something big going on down there. So we don't want to louse up their chances with anything the wop sends out. I'll leave it to you, Lippincott, since you found him, and, besides, I've got my hands full with the party here. But don't fuck it up, Lippincott. There are so many less agreeable places I can think of for you like . . . ' he wandered over, still scrabbling at his fairy-lights, to the map on his wall. 'Cape Wrath? . . . Baffin Island? . . . '

'Antarctica? . . . '

'Sounds promising. But I ask myself if even that might not be unduly lenient.'

17

The boys were playing navies in the stream at the end of the rockery in the half-hour or so before bedtime.

Rufus was the British Navy and Adam was the French Fleet in Morocco, and the game consisted chiefly in Rufus aiming a spring-loaded trench mortar filled with tiny pebbles at Adam's quirkily assorted and unfairly vulnerable command: a Bakelite rowing-boat, a couple of metal motor-launches which never worked and a tin trawler with the hatches ripped off — none of which could possibly be considered a threat to Rufus's large and stoutly-constructed *King George V*.

'You can scuttle the trawler if you like,' said Rufus, generously.

He was having more than ordinary trouble despatching it.

But Adam was tired.

The sky had clouded over slightly but the evening was still oppressively warm, and he felt hot, sticky and bad-tempered. It had been a yo-yo of a day, full of crests and troughs, but he didn't see why he should end it in defeat – for Lucy's sake as much as anybody else. So he took a lump of earth from the bank, and hurled it at his brother's pugnacious dreadnought, scoring an absolute corker of a hit. The vessel meekly turned over and sank, along with its weaponry and several jolly sailors.

Rufus was absolutely furious, but as usual his rage didn't begin with a show of physical force.

'So you want to see the Frights tonight, do you?'

'I . . . I don't believe in the Frights.'

'The Frights believe in you. They believe in you very strongly. They're looking for a little boy tonight. And now you've made me angry and I don't see why I should stand in their way. You know what that means, don't you? Don't you?'

'I don't see why I should always have to lose.'

'I'm the eldest son. The eldest son can't lose. Granny says that. It's the law of Cutcombe. Now jolly well get in and pick everything up, including the crew, or I'll definitely decide against giving you the you-know-what tonight.'

Adam was standing there, flush-faced and poised between rebellion and dismay like the Apostate Seraph whom the Reverend Biddle had so vividly described in his sermon on Loyalty, when there was a call from Nanny, and they both hurriedly gathered up the combined naval strengths of the Mediterranean Station.

'Will you give me the Sleeping Draught tonight?' said Adam, dismay asserting itself as they hurried back to the house.

'That depends,' said Rufus, loftily.

'Depends on what?'

'Come here at once, you two,' cried Nanny at the door.

She was looking flushed and harassed, her hair was coming down over her eyes, her forehead was glistening, and her starched apron heaved like a pontoon over an Atlantic swell. It had been a rush to ride back and get changed, but she had found time to put Mrs Nethercott's potion into her little cupboard, and turn the key. She didn't know if she was brave enough to take it yet.

'It's long past your suppertime,' she said. 'Go and say goodnight to your Granny, and then get straight up those stairs.'

The boys trailed along the verandah, down the passage past the cloakroom where the boats were kept, peculiarly flavoured with gun-cleaners and oilskins, and on through the grownups' hall with the elephant-tusk gong outside the dining-room, and the grandfather clock that told the tides, and the tiger on the wall that great-grandfather had shot in India, and the prints of Sarah Siddons in her most dramatic roles, and into the drawing-room where Granny and Chell sat like the masks of Tragedy and Comedy.

Chell was feeling pleased with life, or at least as near pleasure as she could get. With the Granny still reeling from her son's disappearance, she knew her moment juste had arrived.

A second telephone call had come through, from Tristram's padre, but it had added little to what they knew. He, the padre, was inclined to take the most lenient view of the matter — it had no doubt been a temporary lapse on Tristram's part, the strains of his calling and so forth — at any rate, someone would be with them at least by tomorrow morning. We must all pray for guidance in these

185

troublous times. Apologies for unpleasant. Click. Silence. Even God was cut off.

The Granny was quite unmanned by this confirmation of the possibility of her son's fall from grace. Somehow the padre's pussy tones made it much more real than the Colonel's blunt communiqué. But she clung to the hope that there had been some mistake.

'There has to be some explanation,' she kept repeating to Chell. 'We at Cutcombe do not swerve from duty. He always jumped his fences straight. I think I'd better have a sherry.'

'Please,' said Chell.

'I beg your pardon.'

'If you want me to get you a sherry, kindly say please.'

'Are you sure you're hearing things properly?' said the Granny, rallying slightly, 'or has your twangling instrument addled your wits? You're clearly not yourself. Hoots toots and awa' wi' ye.'

'I'm all right,' said Chelly-Chops, 'it's you that's got the problem. You couldn't see the Day of Judgement even if the graves were being vacated, under your nose. You're so full of your stage here . . . ' she swept a comprehensive arm round to denote the Cutcombe Estate. 'You can't see out into the real world at all. The facts are plain. Your son, poor fellow, is a sham, a cardboard character, a pretty façade covering a multitude of structural defects who wouldn't fool anyone except you and an Army Medical Board. And that's your fault. You put him on his pedestal and now he's fallen off. I'm only surprised it took him so long. He's not best. He never has been best. He's a ramshackle mess like the rest of us.'

The Granny made vague flapping gestures to disassociate herself from any such vulgar implication.

'How can you say these things to me? Have you no heart, Chell? My sheep is lost,' she said, switching her tack. 'Oh Absalom, my son, my son.'

186

'I had forgotten the Jewish connection.'

The Granny gave her a ghastly look. This must go no further.

'Have I been nursing a viper in my bosom?'

'Oh, he'll turn up. Like the proverbial penny. Probably sooner. He can't come to much harm in Devonshire. He couldn't drown in a bog. He's much too lightweight.'

'Stop. Stop. This is disgraceful. Chelford, go to your room.'

'But we're evading the issue. I wish to speak about the rest of your "stage". It's not a pretty sight, and only you could fail to see it. But let me be your eyes. Your daughter-in-law, who at least knows exactly what your son is, persists in having louche assignations with Americans all over the Estate.'

'I won't listen.'

'Louche, I say. I saw her with my own eyes capering naked on the Quarry. Like something worse than Greek.'

'Ohh,' the Granny covered her ears.

'The Italian sleeps with the village girls. And his wife is having an affair with . . . guess who?'

'I don't . . . I won't . . . '

'I fear the evidence is conclusive.' Chell produced Tristram's missing letter to Griselda. 'The place is a cesspit.'

The Granny reached out a wavering hand and held the letter as if it had been something precious found in a drain.

'Even the children are affected,' Chell pursued. 'Why even this morning before lunch . . . '

But at this moment, right on cue, Adam and Rufus entered.

They hated this part of the daily ritual because the Granny was not someone one really felt happy about kissing. It was not that she was in any way old-smelling or ill-favoured, in fact, in her day, she had been deeply admired, but she had for so long pursued the way of authority and tartness that embracing her was like balancing on the edge of an acid bath. But anyway, they kissed her and it appeared to restore some of her strength.

'There they are, Chell. These are the wicked monsters. I must say, they look pretty evil to me. Eh, Adam?'

She playfully boxed him on the ear. He turned, embarrassed, and she boxed him harder on the other one.

'Turn the other cheek, that's the ticket,' she chortled, roguishly.

He almost preferred it when she was being cross.

'Tell us that story, Rufus,' she went on, encouraging them to linger while she worked out what to do about Chelford — she couldn't get rid of her, the woman knew too much — but she would punish her. 'That one about Jesus in your heart.'

This was an old favourite of the Granny's, and everyone had heard it more times than they cared to remember, but Rufus didn't mind feeding her the lines once more as the story reflected credit on himself.

'It was with our Nanny before this.'

'The temporary one they had before,' said the Granny to Chell, who was watching the proceedings with an enigmatic smile. 'She was a Plymouth Brethren or something equally fervent, and she was always talking about people who had Jesus in their heart. Well, one day, we had Lord and Lady St Paget over to tea here, and Rufus came down and was introduced. Lady St Paget had for some reason that day an awfully rumbly tummy. Anyway, when Rufus had been introduced, he came up very close to her and said very gravely . . . tell us what you said, Rufus?'

'I said, "Have you got Jesus in your heart?" '

'Lady St Paget looked surprised, but rallied well and said yes, she hoped she had. And then . . . tell us . . . what did you say, Rufus?'

'I said I thought so because I could hear him grunting.'

The Granny, in spite of her trials that day or perhaps because of them, shook and shook with laughter, and

Chell, for all the strength of her hand, began to look a little less like Mrs Nethercott's Luttrell after a bowl of cream.

'Hahahaha. Hear him grunting. Wasn't it priceless? Hear him grunting,' she kept crowing, 'wasn't it simply priceless?'

Her recovered spirits encouraged Adam to try a little narration of his own. He didn't see why Rufus should have all the limelight and, if grunting were a subject of amusement, he had a little grunting story of his own.

'This time,' he said, 'it's Nanny that does the grunting.'

There was a sudden silence which, for once, Adam failed to interpret as ominous.

Chell perked up, sensing something useful to her cause. Granny cocked her head one side, her instinct for Adam-detection pinging like an Asdic, but at the same time aware that this might not be the moment to indulge it. And Rufus, anticipating what his brother was about to divulge, gave him a glance that would have caused Medusa herself to file a suit for loss of earnings. But Adam had eyes only for the limelight.

Curiosity got the better of Granny's sense of caution.

'Well, well, Adam,' she said enticingly. 'Tell us about Nanny and her funny noises.'

'It was when she was in the stables with Rodgers.'

'With Rodgers? Yes?'

Chell leaned forwards with light of victory in her eyes, turning her instrument up to max so she wouldn't miss a syllable of Adam's revelation.

'She was grunting in the stables with Rodgers?' elucidated Granny.

'Yes.'

'They were playing at piggies to amuse you, perchance?'

'It wasn't for us.'

'Us? You were there too eh, Rufus?'

Rufus shot another urgent warning signal at Adam as he answered.

'Sort of. By mistake.'

189

'This gets stranger and stranger. Well, Adam, continue. What were they doing?'

'They were lying on the straw and pushing at each other and . . . grunting . . . '

The Granny, too late, saw the trap that, in her relentless pursuit of her grandson's character-formation, she had walked straight into. She ground her teeth.

Chell was almost uncontrollable with triumph.

'That's quite enough, Adam.'

'But she was grunting, Granny.'

'So you say, Adam, so you say. But grunting is not, I think, a subject we wish to pursue. I think we have had quite enough grunting for one day.'

Adam could not imagine why his story had fallen so flat, but was prepared to leave it at that, when Chell intervened, sensing that there was still more discomfiture to be extracted from the situation.

'And when, at what hour, did this all take place, Adam?'

'It was . . . '

Suddenly the full realization of his indiscretion swept over him. In pursuit of the bubble of applause, he had taken a forbidden path. Rufus would never forgive him for so great a tale-telling. And it was nearly night. Adam looked desperately round the room, but help came neither from the east nor from the west.

'Yes? We are waiting, Adam.'

'It was dark. I was at the window. I didn't know they'd be there.'

'It was you, Rufus, wasn't it?' Chell fixed him with her malevolent twinkly eyes. 'You took your brother down to the stables to watch your Nanny grunting with Rodgers, when you should both have been in bed?'

It was a question that did not require an answer. All four people in the room, though normally grouped in some sort of pattern of alliances, were separated by unfathomable distance.

Chell debated whether to bring up the subject of Lucy in the laurels, which she had happened to observe that morning, more by judgement than luck, but decided she already had laurels enough for the moment.

There was a grave silence.

'I think you had better go to bed now,' said Granny. 'I shall decide on your punishment in the morning. And tell Nanny I should like a word with her if you please. And I don't want you to mention this matter to anyone. Do you understand? If this got out . . . '

Chell looked triumphant.

There was no 'Good night' as the boys trudged from the room. Rufus did not speak to Adam as they mounted the stairs to the nursery, and a gathering cargo of pebbles in his stomach made each step heavier than the last. From the look on Rufus's face, he couldn't disguise from himself the likelihood that he wouldn't be qualifying for the Sleeping Draught tonight. His mother would be out, Nanny would be in the doghouse or quite possibly back with her family at the Mill, and there'd be no one, absolutely no one, to look after him at all.

'Nanny, Granny wants to see you in the drawing-room,' Rufus told her.

'Whatever for?'

'Adam told her you were in the stables with Rodgers.'

Nanny didn't stop to ask how he knew.

'What you want to do that for?'

'I thought it was going to make her laugh.'

'Oh. You.'

Nanny sat down and burst into tears. The spectacle of a grownup crying was both shocking and faintly ridiculous. The trouble with grownups was that there was so much of them, and when they cried, it seemed, they couldn't help overdoing it, massive oozings, not neat little tears like Lucy's would've been. Oh Lucy.

He really didn't understand how anyone sensible could

love a big girl. He did feel sorry for Nanny, and guilty too, but there was only a limited amount of concern he could give, his main care being for the night which was closing on him faster than he could run, like the tide at Blue Anchor.

'I'm sorry, Nanny. I didn't mean to.'

Rufus turned and looked at him coldly, speaking directly to him for the first time.

'Now look what you've done,' he said. 'You're not just a traitor, you're cruel as well.'

'I'm sorry. I didn't mean to. Sorry,' he pleaded.

'I'm sorry too. But I know some people who'll be glad. People who look this way and that . . . ' he gave a peculiarly accurate impression of a predatory reptile.

Adam was appalled.

'Nanny . . . Rufus isn't going to give me any Sleeping Draught,' he said.

But Nanny had too much of her own to think about. Beside she had taken some of Mrs Nethercott's mixture and was beginning to feel most peculiar.

'Leave me alone and go to bed,' she said, rushing to her room to put a brush through her hair.

So, later, when the Mother came in before she went off to the party looking good enough to eat but distant in pale-blue silk and smelling of Stephanotis, and bent low over the bed to give him his kiss-ration, he tried it on her too.

'Mummy, Rufus won't give me my Sleeping Draught tonight.'

But she told him it was nonsense and they shouldn't even play games about such things, and why had they been upsetting everyone downstairs. She'd really have to think about sending them both away to school.

And, when she had gone, Rufus gave his little odd smile, turned his face to the wall, and refused to speak, even though Adam got increasingly desperate.

18

The band was playing selections from *Showboat* and Thomas, smoking a Camel, sipping a little scotch, looked round with some satisfaction.

The music was passable, the old bivouac mess-tent, proofed for blackout looked really rather elegant (the Major's finally-unravelled fairy lights lending a certain end-of-pier twinkle), the buffet groaned with all the victuals the Americans seemed to have in profusion but which the ordinary locals hadn't seen for years (a party at the Base was worth attending for the beef alone), he was in love, and he was about to pull off the first and quite possibly the only coup of his career, military or otherwise.

He had checked that the jeep was fuelled and that his service automatic was loaded and functioning — not, he felt, that he would need it with Franco who, though an enemy agent, was still a kind of friend, even though he *had* been a creep at that dinner-party.

The Major had offered assistance but Thomas had declined it, saying that it would only alert Franco that something was up if he were shadowed by heavies. It would be better, in the unlikely event of any crisis tonight, to leave it to someone who knew the man.

As for himself, he reflected, if he had to bring Franco in, he wanted to do it in style, in a manner fitting both the artist and the hero. Hero? Yes, surely that was his role. Love, which softened men of teak, had turned him into a lion.

But a funny sort of lion, he thought, a somewhat unlikely lion. He was very willing to play the part but at the same time he knew it couldn't be serious. A lion in a den of Daniels. Or as if I'm playing two parts at once, half lion and half lamb. There seemed at times to be a serious difference of opinion between the Author and the Casting Director.

The Major had shrugged and given him one of his wry oeillades.

Anyway, everything was fine now, just fine, so fine in fact, that he was having difficulty controlling his leonine expression. It would keep lapsing into a goofy grin.

He went to the john and adjusted his expression again, coming out with a sneer of cold command that would have looked well on Tiglath-pileser the Assyrian. It lapsed into fatuity again when he thought he saw Julia near the bar – but it was only Mrs Luttrell, after whose immemorial family Mrs Nethercott's cat drew his name.

The guests were starting to arrive.

He made attempts at conversation and even one or two small jokes to various local dignitaries who scurried in eagerly, their eyes on the beef, but all the while his eyes were on the door.

Quarter past. Half past. Nearly quarter to, and the edge was beginning to come off his optimism, when suddenly she was there, laughing over her shoulder at something Franco was saying.

Thomas's brow darkened momentarily. Perhaps he wouldn't mind taking the man in after all, and not civilizedly, with a certain amount of casual banter, but dragged through the streets behind his Willys to the derision of the populace.

He had rather hoped anyway, forgetting the necessary economies of rationing, that she might have been able to come separately, so they could have had a little time together before his shadowing duties began.

But he let none of this show in his features as he hurried over to the Cutcombe party.

'Bang, bang,' he said to her, indicating a positive reaction to her dress. 'I'm dead.'

'My son has just told me I look as good as a Rice Krispie.

I think he meant to eat, though it could have had a moral connotation.'

'Haha.'

The gathering all had a good laugh.

'I like Rice Krispies. In fact, I love Rice Krispies.'

'Like a good Yank.'

He didn't like her calling him a Yank, but he didn't let it show for one moment.'

'Say hello to Griselda and Franco,' she said.

'Hello, Griselda and Franco.'

Perhaps she was slightly drunk. Perhaps they were all slightly drunk. Griselda certainly looked pale.

'Hello, Lieutenant,' Griselda said.

Chell had wasted no time in telling her about Tristram's disappearance, and she was surprised how much the news affected her – a great deal more than that cow of a wife who had just said airily 'Oh, he'll turn up', as Chell had done, 'no one dies in Devonshire.' What an idiot he was. Not a romantic ruin at all as she'd first thought. Just a ruin pure and simple. What a mess it all was. Perhaps the crumpet-face had been right all along. She'd have been better off with a pippin-cheeked squire.

'What can I get you to drink?' the mooning Lieutenant was saying.

'A lot.'

'Now, Zelda,' said Franco, 'that is not nice, that is not, how you say, nicely brought up. You see, Lieutenant, what a hard time she gives me. I shall tell your crumpet-faced mother, Zelda, and she shall slap your wrists. Notty girl. Two big whiskies, thank you, Lieutenant.'

'And a gin and lime for me, darling,' said Julia, brightly.

There was no doubt about it. She wasn't the same person she had been this afternoon. Her words rose up, her heart remained below. She sounded cordial, almost effusive, but her eyes were restless.

What is it about parties that brings out the worst in pretty

195

women, Thomas wondered. It's like an old hunter hearing the horn. View halloo and they're off. But surely he was the only fox, the only conceivable fox after the closeness of the afternoon?

As if in answer to his question, Major Chuck now made his appearance among the group, greeting the girls with what seemed to Thomas quite unnecessary familiarity, and giving Franco a hearty 'Buon giorno'.

'Everything tickety-boo?' he enquired facetiously of Julia.

Thomas winced. Really, one doesn't have to guy the British to their faces. (How could she even endure five minutes with the crass fellow?) Nobody else seemed to mind, however.

'The Lieutenant here looking after you all right? He's a great looker-after, aren't you, Lieutenant? Tell 'em about the time in April when you looked after that transport exercise and you had the whole column stuck down a narrow lane with no turning-place, and the last truck got a wheel in the ditch so we couldn't even back up out. In the end we had to get a couple of carthorses to lend a little weight to the occasion. That looked after a whole day for us. An evening for our friend the Lieutenant should be a bagatelle. But watch out you don't get bogged down all the same.'

Everyone had a good laugh, in which Thomas of course joined, but he couldn't fail to notice the challenge in the Major's voice and wondered if everyone else were noticing it too. He wished the Major triple hernia.

'Tell 'em about the time . . . ' the Major continued.

But Thomas decided the thing had gone far enough. He wasn't going to stand by and be turned into a buffoon.

'Certainly, Major. But maybe they've come to enjoy themselves, not to hear military smalltalk.'

This was perhaps indiscreet of him. The Major's eyes narrowed dangerously, but widened again when Julia took his arm and led him away across the marquee.

'I adore military gossip,' she said. 'All those lovely men. I want to hear all about your activities on and off the field.'

Thomas thought he would never understand women. How could the girl who had so privately played Primavera with him this afternoon suddenly leave him so publicly in the lurch?

'I tell you why,' said Franco, more kindly, reading his expression, which was now in serious need of further adjustment. 'It is because she is afraid. She does not want, how you say, all the eggs in one basket. She does not want one big egg in one big basket. She needs caviare on a lot of little toasts. That is her nature.'

'What nonsense you talk, Franco,' said Griselda, the alcohol making her quarrelsome; then, addressing herself to Thomas. 'The Latin understanding of women is the world's biggest myth. The Italians simply put a halo round Lechery by calling it Romance. On the subject of women, I am here to tell you,' she swayed slightly, 'an Italian accent is not necessarily a passport to the truth. The truth is . . .'
She paused portentously as an orderly filled her glass. 'The truth is that we are like trees and men are so much wind. We dance in the breeze, we bend in the gale, but if we believe you too much, if we try and join your world of air, we uproot and destroy ourselves. Men think we're inconstant, but it's their fault for giving us all that hot air. Certainly we bend from side to side. But at bottom we remain firm.'

It was clear that Griselda was more than slightly drunk. And at bottom she didn't seem to be very firm at all. Franco and Thomas exchanged glances of masculine commiseration.

'You forget, Zelda,' he said gently. 'You forget that I have no passport at all — to the truth or to anything else.'

Thomas wished he hadn't said that. The more he saw of the man, the more he was beginning to like him. What did they do with enemy agents in wartime? He had an uncomfortable feeling it was something rather terminal.

'Would you like something to eat?' he suggested, beginning not to enjoy this evening at all and suddenly torn
between his escort duties and his desire to go and revive the
tendernesses of the afternoon with Julia. There could only
be the smallest of misunderstandings.

At the buffet, a bevy of well-bred English faces was to be
found, all trying not to drool as thick slices of broiled steak
were heaped onto outstretched plates. But Julia's was not
among them.

He left Griselda and Franco in the queue (he would surely
not slip away in the proximity of steak) and hurried back to
the bar. There was no sign of her. Nor was she on the
dance-floor, which was deserted except for the camp cat.

He returned to the buffet with a growing feeling of
unease in his stomach which the broiled flesh Franco had
collected for him did nothing to alleviate.

He tried not to think of Franco's flesh − dead − on a
slab. Or Julia's − enmeshed with another man's −
gloriously alive.

'Cheer up,' said Griselda, hiccuping. 'You're not dead
yet.'

It was a phrase he had always found detestable. He
rather thought he was going to need another of his pills.

19

In the darkness, Adam could hear nothing but the beating
of his heart.

He had tried with all his might to fall asleep without the
Draught, but sleep wouldn't come.

The trouble with counting sheep jumping over stiles was

that, however soothing they seemed at first, you slowly became aware of a sense of panic among the animals, that they weren't just lolloping after Nod the Shepherd in a twilight dim with rose but were scrambling feverishly, eyes wide with terror, fighting bloodily for safety, aware of something huge and unbearably horrible behind them like Miss Muffet's spider big as a child.

So he gave that up too, along with all the other patent ways he had learned to bring sleep after lunch, like blipping the pompom of the light cord, or getting under the bed-clothes and pretending the bed was a submarine. It wasn't going anywhere tonight.

He had tried to imagine what it would be like, where the Frights would take him and what they would do. Rufus had never given him a full catalogue of the actual details. They needed little boys. But what for? Would they train him in horribleness and give him loathsome warts like Vera Brewster's mother who lived in Allercombe, so he'd eventually turn into a Fright himself, or would he just be their servant to run their evil errands, fed on scraps and sleeping in corners? Or would they simply cut out his heart and eat it for their dinner — a Cutcombe heart, singularly toothsome.

He had tried to make Rufus relent, he had begged and begged, but this time he had gone too far, Rufus said. Not only had he laid the blame on him for taking him down to the stables, but he had committed the final sin of telling the grownups about the Sleeping Draught. The fact that no one had paid any attention didn't make any difference. There was only one punishment for that.

He had tried Nanny's room at the bottom of the corridor, but it was locked and, if she *was* there, she wasn't answering.

At last a kind of tired resignation had fallen on him. Like picking the figs and breaking the window with Field Marshal Ball and giggling in church when the Reverend

Biddle told them (with singular lack of success) to larve one anarther, he was guilty and he had to be punished. He even found himself willing them to come, now, to get it over with.

Out in the woods, a pheasant wailed. A floorboard creaked in the corridor. Somewhere deep in the house a clock struck ten.

Time for little boys to be asleep.

He lay rigid in his bed and waited.

20

In his hiding-place among the trees, Tristram knew that the hour had come. It was time to make contact. Pushing aside the old oil-cloth he had been using as a blanket, he staggered to his feet and walked stiffly over to the darkest corner where, underneath a clutch of rotten logs, he had stored the woodcutter's axe. It wasn't a very good axe. Indeed, the woodsman had probably left it there because he had no further use for it. It was chipped in the head and splintered about the haft. But it made Tristram feel he wasn't entirely unarmed, and gave him a certain precarious confidence as he crept among the firs.

There was light enough for him to see his path without making him too easy a target.

The shadows seemed to have gone from his mind, which was encouraging. He knew exactly where he was and what he had to do. He simply hoped his contact in the cave would be similarly on the qui vive.

He suddenly emerged from the forest onto a small clearing above a steeply banked metalled road. He was starting to make a ginger descent when at the point of no return he saw the distant glimmer of an approaching vehicle. He slid down the bank, raced across the lane, and scrambled feverishly up the further side, throwing himself through the hedge as a lorry came wheezing past.

He found himself in a field of cows who gazed at him with large and gentle eyes. They didn't seem to mind that he wasn't all he was cracked up to be. In fact, he thought he could detect something akin to relief on their faces as they peered at him ruminatively through the gloaming.

'You're absolutely right,' he said to them, 'it's better to vegetate. Just got to see this little lot through,' he gestured confidingly at his axe as though it explained everything. 'And then I'm your man.'

The cows appeared to appreciate his point and stirred about gravely among the buttercups.

As he traversed the spinney on the other side of the pasture, a memory of school echoed in his mind, Squarey and he singing in *The Pirates of Penzance*.

> With cat-like tread upon our prey we steal
> In silence dread, our cautious way we feel . . .

And, what was it? 'Poor Wandering One'.

The end was nearly in sight.

He wished he had that Browning automatic he'd been issued with, it would help now in the event of a patrol; but hadn't they said in training, 'Nothing ever works out quite the way you think — always be ready to improvise'? Gunfire would alert the Jerries anyway. He had the ideal weapon right here in his hand. The only thing was, he didn't know if he'd be able to use it. Make your decision and act fast, that's what the manual said. He'd never had to kill a man.

They were all looking at him to see if he would fail. Squarey and Ferdy Fowler, the Brigadier, Griselda, his wife, his mother.

Come along now, Master Tristram, quick's the word and sharp's the action.

21

The dance-floor was crowded now, but Thomas as he miserably piloted Griselda in a foxtrot, could still keep Franco under reasonable supervision. He was sitting with an Air Force Colonel making simian gestures which appeared to be evoking uncontrollable mirth.

Griselda was more tractable after her meal, and her bottom had become almost ominously flexible as they danced.

'I'm sorry I was cross,' she said, 'it's just that the war's such a no-man's-land. You know? One can't get on with anything. It's all very well for men. But all we can do is make munitions and drop our knickers. It's like standing on the touchline being expected to cheer and give people lemons at halftime.'

Thomas could see some justice in her argument, but he still couldn't see Julia. He let go of Griselda and her lemons, and mopped his brow as the band played a loud and terminating chord, followed by another more annunciatorial.

'Ladies and gentlemen, there will now be a short exhibition of Morris Dancing by Mr Georgie Taylor and the West Somerset Mummers . . . introduced by . . . .the Reverend Biddle.'

There was a sporadic outburst of enthusiasm.

'Deah friends, fellow-countrymen, welcome visitors to our shores . . . As you may or may not know, these ha dances stem from the most immemorial antiquitah . . . '

'It's kind of hot,' he said. 'Why don't we grab a drink and walk around outside a little?'

This was perhaps mildly indiscreet, in so far as Franco just might take the opportunity of slipping off. But he didn't look in the slightest bit as though he were contemplating a skedaddle, and besides, there were the Morris Dancers to consider. He wouldn't, even if details of Winston Churchill's secret movements for the next four months were on offer, miss the opportunity of witnessing such a priceless exhibition of the English facility for the grotesque.

They wandered over to the bar, grabbed a couple of scotches, and strolled out into the night as the accordion and the fiddle struck up 'Quantock Dandy'.

The sky was still clear overhead but great malignant cauliflower clouds were building up westwards, out at sea, and there were subdued mutterings in the air and flickers of light on the horizon as though somebody had lit the whole thing like a glass of sambuca.

Griselda suddenly drew him to her and kissed him hard on the mouth.

The evening was taking the form of a most extraordinary sort of nightmare, Thomas reflected. Not that being kissed by Griselda was unpleasant, but it just wasn't the sort of thing that he could conceive of happening. Reality was clearly slipping its shackles. The next thing that happened was more nightmarish still.

There was a sound in the air that Thomas had at first taken for another thundery rumble. But it went on. And grew louder. And as it came closer he was able to distinguish what it was.

'A bomber,' he said. 'One . . . two . . . Just two of them.'

'Some of yours?' Griselda asked.

'I guess so,' he said, but there was something about them that evoked memories of the lecture he'd attended on aircraft

203

recognition. 'No . . . wait a min . . . *GET THAT LIGHT OUT OVER THERE.*'

There was a flurry of activity as the blackout round the entrance to the mess tent was adjusted, and then a terrible moment of powerlessness followed.

The first two hit-and-run Heinkels passed low overhead, banked slightly towards the sea and passed straight over the little port. And suddenly the night was full of the banshee whistle and detonation of bombs, followed by the muffled thumps and crumps of things exploding.

Thomas pushed Griselda roughly to the ground and was about to rush back into the tent when another two bombers appeared out of the east, heading straight for the camp.

The first dropped its load on the parade ground, firing a few huts and generally disfiguring the tarmac. The second, piloted by a cheerful baritone, deposited its stick along the officers' living quarters, right next to the mess tent itself.

The noise was so appallingly larger than life that, for what seemed like a light year, Thomas just lay there without movement.

Finally, he noticed he was groaning. Not because he was hurt – at any rate, he could feel no damage – but because groaning seemed to be the only possible reaction to such an event.

He reached across to Griselda and shook her arm. She didn't move. A thin trickle of blood was coming out of her mouth, and he noticed there was a large discoloured hole in her rather pretty cream dress just above her waist.

Poor Griselda, he thought. It was full time now. The clock had run out.

From the direction of the tent came mingled cries of pain and confusion.

Looking about him with shock and disbelief, Thomas took in a horrifying scene of carnage. It was as if a harmless picture of merrymaking and pleasure had been defaced by a warped delinquent.

Amid the shattered wreckage of the tent, carnation and

geranium petals floated like confetti over an excremental smearing of vermilion. Vermilion across tablecloths, frocks, tuxedos, service-dresses, vermilion across masters of fox-hounds, justices of the peace, landed gentry, lawyers, parsons, persons of debatable origin, ladies of limited means, and even a few veteran gatecrashers from as far away as Bridgwater.

The cream of West Somerset society lay there flecked with obscene ketchup.

Thomas spotted Lady St Paget insensible, being tended by her shocked Lord who held a napkin to a gaping head wound.

He saw the Reverend Biddle staring incredulously at the mangled stump of his hand while the Mummers lay about him in absurd and pathetic postures like broken puppets.

He saw the Colonel who had been laughing at Franco's antics, still baring his teeth because most of his jaw had been blown away.

But he couldn't see Julia. Or Major Chuck. Or Franco . . .

'Thomas . . . Thomas . . . Wake up. You look as though you've seen a ghost.'

What was this?

Thomas looked round. Everything, just as it had been before the attack, swam back into his vision. No blood, no mangled stumps, the tent upright on its pins.

Griselda was standing in front of him wagging a reproving finger.

'We've all had rather a lot,' she said, 'but that's no reason to go glassy-eyed.'

What hellish phantasm had he been allowed to see? Had it happened? Was it about to happen? Whatever it was, he felt surprisingly unsurprised. Maybe it had been a warning. If Franco had been sending messages, he could have communicated their exact position. The carnage could be yet to come.

He ran back and looked through the entrance at where

Franco had been sitting. There was no sign of him. The Colonel sat by himself sticking his jaw into a large glass of beer.

'Thomas . . . for Christ's sake come and dance,' Griselda said, peevishly.

He ran to the Major's room and banged on the door.

'Go away.'

He banged some more.

'Major, this is urgent.'

'Get the fuck out of here.'

'Major, this is a matter of security.'

Finally, after a long pause, the door inched open. The Major was half-dressed and struggling with his belt.

'What the hell's going on? This had better be important, Lippincott.'

Beyond him, Thomas knew what he was going to see, had known, it seemed to him, all evening, but it was still more shattering than his vision of the bombs, more painful than anything he could ever have imagined experiencing. It seemed to turn his heart inside out like a rubber-duck.

Julia was half-sitting, half-lying in the bed, clutching a green service shirt to her curiously-diminished nakedness, and looking inglorious and frightened. Was this part of the nightmare too?

He pushed past the Major into the room.

'What the hell?' said the Major.

'Thomas . . . don't . . . ' said Julia, and started to weep.

Of course, it couldn't be happening.

'Each man kills the thing he loves,' said Thomas, 'but a woman does it quicker.'

'Now see here . . . ' said the Major.

'He's gone,' said Thomas, 'and I'm going out to look for him. But there's no need for you to be disturbed. The best thing for you to do is to carry on with what you're doing. And then, when you've fucked everything else around

206

here, you can go and fuck yourself.'

And he turned and ran out into the night for his jeep as the rain started to fall, thick and slow, like arterial blood.

22

His way took him past the guest carpark and, as he ran he was just in time to see the Cutcombe Wolseley vanishing through the guard gates with an uncharacteristic squealing of rubber. Something made him pause for a moment to inspect the space it had vacated, and he noted in the beam of his flashlight that the rain was spreading a blood-red blur over the gravel, indicating that Franco himself had not escaped unscathed.

Thomas ran on, located the Willys and, shouting unintelligible admonitions to a bewildered guard, drove headlong towards the hills.

Ten minutes of precarious hurtling through the rain brought him to the track he had reconnoitred that afternoon. Here he parked the jeep and proceeded on foot. He had no need of caution now, for the tempo of the rain had suddenly increased from its earlier solemn Grave to a hectic Furioso, turning the path into a stream which appeared to be running red as the rivers of Egypt (though whether it was Somerset earth or Italian blood he did not stop to establish).

Arriving with doused torch at the thicket in front of Franco's hide, at last he paused and collected his breath.

It was difficult to believe that only seven hours before he had been lying naked, a hundred yards or so away, happier than he had ever been in his life. It seemed like another existence. In fact, he was beginning to believe it was. It was the only thing that could explain the extraordinary discrep-

ancies in, for instance, Julia's behaviour, the sudden lurches from violence to junketing that he had just witnessed down at the Camp. His awareness was being switched between two strands of Time. How it was happening or why it should be happening to him were questions he would have to consider later. The problem at the moment was to try and determine Original Time, Time One, from the nightmare Time Two which kept encroaching, which kept seeping and infiltrating like the memories which haunted him, and indeed at times seeming to merge with that odious and familiar darkness from his past.

Whichever Time it was, however, the moment was too pressing for delay. Peeping through the curtain of undergrowth, he surveyed the tunnel within. If it was Franco who had provided the idea of the Frights living here, there was a certain macabre irony in the scene that was revealed.

Franco was clawing at the packing-case where the transmitter was stored, but there was a dark arterial ooze coming from a shredded patch of shirt just above his abdomen, and he didn't seem to be doing too well. Thomas, in spite of his previous rage, was just about to step in and help him (which would, of course, have been ridiculous), when with a supreme and blood-welling effort, he lifted it onto the small trestle table.

He rested for a moment or two, breathing heavily, and Thomas could sense the mistiness filling the channels of his thoughts like the vapours of his beloved Venice.

Franco now tapped out a call-sign, then paused, appearing uncertain about the actual content of the message.

'Murdering bastards. I wish you in hell with all the oil-wells of Ploesti up your arse,' he muttered, but appeared dissatisfied, as if the communiqué might not contain quite the right degree of panache.

'Adolph Hitler wears women's underclothes.'

Too schoolboyish.

Ah, this was better.

'The only thing to be said for Art is that it places men a little closer to the angels than their conduct would otherwise suggest.'

Too good for them, of course, but . . .

At this point, he noticed Thomas standing at the entrance, covering him with an automatic.

'Lieutenant Lippincott . . . ' he smiled weakly. 'Shoot if you want to. It would be doing me a considerable service.'

'Why?' said Thomas, 'why did you do it?'

'They had my mother. I did not know they would do this. But now anyway I believe my mother is dead. They were simply using me. They have put her in a camp and . . . '

'Griselda is dead too.'

Franco made a choking noise that was half grief and half blood.

'Surely,' said Thomas — his anger had vanished completely now and he could only feel pity for the man — 'surely you could've seen . . . '

'Ah, my friend,' said Franco, 'I was blind. Some artist, eh? I did not wish to let the truth come between me and my hopes. And now I . . . '

His head drooped for a moment, and then he looked up and a curious expression came into his eyes.

Thomas turned to examine the object of his gaze, and for a fraction of a second, saw a bearded tatterdemalion looming up out of the darkness behind, swinging an axe at him. Warned by Franco's glance, he ducked instinctively, and the blow wobbled in its descent and only half struck home.

Thomas fell down and watched the proceedings with a sort of dim, sick intermittence.

Redly, he saw the figure stumble forward into the circle of light.

'Sully?' it kept shouting urgently at Franco, 'Sully?'

Some instinct of tidiness in Franco apparently caused him, though mortally wounded, to wish to expire with his head on his shoulders, so when he saw no signs of a halt in the *lunatic's shambling progress, he took the revolver from Thomas's outstretched hand, and shot the intruder square in the chest.*

He went down with a sigh of total astonishment.

'Sully,' he repeated, 'Non, vous vous êtes trompé. Je suis l'Anglais que vous attendiez. Je vous ai sauvé du Gestapo,' gesturing at Thomas.

And then he was quiet for a bit.

'Squarey,' he said, finally, 'turn the lights on . . . Don't be a cad . . . Was that all right, sir? Mother . . . do you read me? I am not receiving you . . . '

Franco, weak though he was, seemed now to recognize the hairy intruder.

'Tristram,' he said softly.

Thomas discerned that it was indeed the formerly-immaculate Captain Sanderson, whom he had cuckolded that very afternoon.

The eyes fluttered and the head turned towards Franco again.

'Who . . . Who's that? Franco? What's going on?'

'I don't know, my friend. But whatever it is, it's not going on much longer.'

Tristram gave a little croaking laugh.

'Don't say I've made a nonsense?'

'Whatever it was you were doing, Tristram and I don't wish to pry into your affairs, it does not look from here like an unqualified success. I am sorry that I shot you. I expect you are sorry that you axed poor Lieutenant Lippincott. He too had bitter sorrows of his own. We have all failed. And death is the ultimate failure. But then one must draw comfort from the fact that it takes as much imagination and talent to fail convincingly as it does to succeed. We have all failed, my friend, but on a tragic scale. Our poet Seneca would certainly have appreciated this little mise en scène.'

Tristram gave a little sigh, tried to say he was sorry, closed

210

his eyes and died.

Franco now, in spite of his words of encouragement, appeared to regard the situation as most unsatisfactory.

'Death', he mumbled, 'could happen to anyone and usually does. For an artist, it comes at the worst possible moment. The last stroke should never introduce the note of cliché.'

At this point something seemed to explode in Thomas's head. A red curtain coming down. Chain reaction? The end? Was that all? A totally unexpected dénouement. The audience didn't seem to like it. There was indeed a sort of roaring noise but a marked absence of applause.

23

'Wake up, wake up,' a jolly voice was saying, and Thomas felt a sharp thump on his back.

In his confusion, he got the impression that he was in on his own birth.

God, he thought, out again already. Is that what they did? Must be a shortage of souls because it's wartime. But you'd think they'd give you time to rest and wash your soul.

> Terrible is the price
> Of beginning anew, of Birth . . .

There you are, he was quoting again. His mind was wearing the same old clothes.

But when he looked reluctantly around, it wasn't a jolly midwife amid scenes of natal bloodletting, it was only

Griselda and the Cutcombe party sitting round a table in the marquee, laughing at him.

'Sometimes we think you're not quite with us,' said young Mrs Sanderson. 'It's not very flattering.'

Thomas felt the back of his head. It appeared to be intact. He couldn't even quite think why he should be surprised at this. He had a sort of memory of blood and faces, but it was all fading fast.

There was only one explanation for it all, he thought, Jung, Donne, Ouspensky, Gödel . . . They would understand. But he doubted very much if it would hold water with the Cutcombeites.

'Do you know anything about quantum theory?' he said.

He looked around. There was the sound of jaws hitting the table. Yes, he had been right in his forecast.

'No, but do tell us, Lippincott,' said the Italian, 'Dic, quam celerrime.'

'The basics of quantum theory rest upon the particle-wave duality of matter . . . '

Griselda made an explosive noise in her glass.

'What it means in terms of Time is that, rather as a beam of light divides when it comes to a choice of, say two holes in a board . . . ' Thomas was floundering, but struggled gamely on ' . . . Time, which can also be regarded as a "wave", divides with every option, that is, with every instant that passes . . . '

He looked round again, helpless in the face of their incomprehension.

'It's an interest of mine,' he explained weakly. 'I was thinking of doing a paper on it with reference to Lewis Carroll.'

They stared at him with a wild surmise.

'Anyway,' he said, 'the theory is, that because of this behaviour of Time, everything that can happen does happen. Somewhere. And what I think has been happening here is . . . we've been living on a fault . . . like Los

Angeles . . . a fault between various strands of Time. I can't tell you why or how. The subject is so new. Electromagnetic disturbance could . . . '

Finally they could contain their mirth no longer and all burst out laughing. It was late and a great deal of liquor had been taken on board. Young Mrs Sanderson (why did he call her this?) was looking particularly beautiful and amused.

'We had one but it died,' she said.

24

There had been thunder earlier, but Adam never minded that. Then there was rain, first torrential and then a soft persistent fall that slithered down pipes and gurgled down gutters, and finally once more the moon had broken through.

Inside the house there was absolute stillness. Just the way it had been in his dream.

First there were the noises, so far away that it seemed they were coming from the moons of Jupiter, and yet not so much far distant as far in, a scratchy whispery sort of noise as though something were trying to get out of a glass dome which had just one little dark hole in it.

He couldn't move. He felt no panic now, just a powerless fascinated painfulness like when he'd had his tonsils out and they'd wheeled him along making jokes he didn't find funny and couldn't laugh at even if he had.

Round and round went the noise. Scratch scratch scratch. They were bound to get out sooner or later, no point in pretending they wouldn't, no point in hoping anything or anyone could stop them.

When the Frights come, Rufus had said it himself, when the Frights come, that's final.

There.

Suddenly, it seemed a connection had been made, a bridge from wherever they were to wherever they were coming which was here, now, right outside, right all around outside his room.

And now it wasn't like his dream any more. The walls, the door, even the ceiling seemed to bulge and dissolve as if the whole room were a cake in a sort of misty baking-tin, and then, and then, whatever it was, whatever they were, they were in the room with him.

And the worst of it was, though he could see quite clearly, he could see nothing. The room looked just the same. But they were here, and a sixth sense told him it was worse, far worse than anything he could possibly have dreamt before. His dreams were human inventions. This was something beyond knowledge, reaching out to him across unimaginable gulfs. And now he screamed, a single anguished cry of utter desolation. But even as he heard himself making the sound, he knew it would reach no one. He was on his own, the web was round him. And even as he thought the words, he saw that he was indeed surrounded now by a sort of swirliness.

And he looked, and he saw that the walls and the ceiling and the screen with Susan and Rover and the picture of Captain Hook the Pirate, and Beales the knitted bear with the puzzled expression and the ears on the side of his head like a man's and even the bit of ribbon Lucy had given him before she got in the car, all of them were being blotted out, snuffed out like nightlights, one by one, so he was left with nothing.

And now he began to feel a sense of spinning, not he himself spinning but round him as though he were in the middle of Rufus's gyro-top. And as he felt this, the worst thing of all started to happen, because he looked at himself and saw he was fading, bits of him were actually vanishing like the Cheshire Cat or like the verdigris when Rodgers poured on the acid from the carboy in the garage.

And he touched his foot and there was nothing. And his knee. And his other arm. And his rib. And there was nothing. Smoke. Emptiness.

And finally he felt his neck, or tried to feel it, but there was nothing there. And he thought in his terror, this can't be right, there won't be anywhere to put my label, no one will know who I am, the Frights must want you for something.

They don't just swallow you up.

And he opened his mouth to scream again. But he found he had no voice to scream with, and, very soon, no mouth to open.

And after that there was nothing at all.

25

Breakfast for the grownups was a formal affair at Cutcombe, and many of them held it to be the best meal of the day.

Not for Granny a plate of cereal followed by a virginal slice of toast. She prided herself, even in wartime, on serving the full Victorian country breakfast with all the trimmings.

You could start with porridge – laced, of course, with Cutcombe cream. And then you could progress to kedgeree, eggs cooked in just about any shape you liked, bacon (without eyes), home-made sausages and even on some occasions devilled kidneys, although these were getting shockingly short, as the mood took you.

The only stipulation (at Cutcombe there were always stipulations) was that however late you had been the night before, it was obligatory to attend before ten o'clock, at which hour Queenie and Amy would take it all away and eat the leftovers.

This particular morning there was a full house for breakfast because Tristram had suddenly turned up.

He had been found, a curious quirk of fate, by Franco, who'd been out cooling his spirit, he said, after the party, on a nocturnal ramble up towards the Old Quarry.

Tristram had appeared from the bushes, somewhat dazed and fatigued and stubbornly reluctant to let go of an old axe-haft he had with him, but otherwise in remarkably fair shape under the circumstances, and had allowed himself to be escorted to the stable flat, where Franco gave him a stiff drink, some food, a bath and a bed.

In the morning, in spite of his ordeal, he had woken not long after his hosts (Franco went over early to the big house to break the news). Tristram had turned down Griselda's offer to breakfast in bed, did not broach the subject of affection, and insisted on presenting himself before the family.

His Unit had now been informed, and the Brigade Medical Officer had been sent over: he was now addressing hismelf to kidneys (the devilled rather than the in situ variety).

The doctor, a Major, a pink-faced man with dark jowls, had indicated that Tristram was suffering from stress following particularly intensive training for a project of the utmost national importance, couldn't tell them exactly what it was of course, but he could say they'd hear all about it in a day or two.

'Rest and quiet,' he said, reverting to Tristram but sucking up to Old Mrs Sanderson through mouthfuls of kidney, 'rest and quiet, can't beat it, wish I could get some myself, frightfully good kidneys. Is that kedgeree over there? There will, of course, following my Report, be absolutely no suggestion of an enquiry.'

Tristram still appeared somewhat restrained. He was polite to his wife, civil to his mother, but seemed on the whole disinclined to enter the general conversation.

At this point, Lieutenant Lippincott drove up from the Camp. He too looked pale and diminuendo. He had come, he said, to return Mrs Sanderson's gold evening bag which she'd left under a table the previous night, to apologize for having been somewhat over the top at the party, and to say goodbye — he was being posted.

The presence of Lippincott seemed to encourage Tristram, and rather to the doctor's annoyance (who felt he should have first refusal on any disclosures), he started to elaborate on his experiences.

'I just . . . went into a sort of blank . . . you know? . . . for a longish sort of spell. But, at the same time, I had the most vivid and, yes, lurid, vision of you all . . . Cutcombe . . . and myself . . . it was like seeing myself but not being part of me . . . You know? . . . And everything was changed . . .'

'Changed?' asked Thomas, roused from thought.

'Sort of recognizable but melted . . . like that bantam in ice they used to have at the Coq d'Or. The stupid thing is, I can't remember any of it now.'

'Classic symptoms, classic symptoms,' said the Doctor, masticating haddock. 'Exactly what one would expect. Perfectly normal.'

But Thomas didn't think it sounded perfectly normal at all. Was there a chance that he wasn't, after all, the only one to be seeing things?

'You didn't happen to get near any lightning, did you?' he asked. 'Globe lightning? An incandescent ball?'

There was a fishbony snort of mirth from the Doctor. Tristram slowly shook his head.

'I don't think so,' he said, 'I really don't remember.'

'No balls,' said the Doctor, sniggering again. 'No balls at all.'

'Why d'you ask?' enquired Tristram.

'It's one of the electro-magnetic conditions in which a man called Gödel suggests a Time-shift could occur. Of course, one could argue that time may be shifting *all* the time. We're simply not aware of it.'

Everyone who'd heard it before looked embarrassed or rolled their eyes, but the Granny gave a peal of scathing laughter. Tristram looked at him with interest.

'Nothing . . . odd's been happening round here, has it?'

Everyone else shook their heads.

'No more than usual. Nothing odd.'

'Apart from Franco's latest abstracts,' said Griselda.

The Italian gave his wife a pretended smite.

'It all started,' Tristram went on, wrinkling his clean-cut features with the effort of memory, 'it all started with this Resistance operation − the doctor here says it was a dummy run to cover every contingency but I thought it was real − that was the point, I suppose. Well, I got myself captured, it was exactly a week ago, early evening, and there was this interrogator, University sort of chap, thought he was very clever, kept talking about Truth and Time . . . and then there was this . . . not your what's it lightning . . . but in my head . . . and then, as I say, I just sort of blanked . . .'

The Italian gave Thomas a glance at that point. Something very distant, the remotest of tintinnabula, seemed to be sounding within him. But the Granny was interrupting. Truth and Time were not subjects she readily countenanced at the breakfast table.

'*Really, dear,*' *she said,* '*I don't think you should even talk about it. You're meant to rest. Ah, and there's little Rufus come to say hello to the hero.*'

The little boy and his Nanny (awkward and whey-faced after a night of the most peculiar sickness and pain − it was

218

*just before dawn when she remembered in half-delirium that
Mrs Rodgers came from Luxborough and might in some
way be related to the witch) were standing at the door.*

'It's all right, Nanny. I know we're not normally allowed
to disturb the grownups at breakfast, but this a special
occasion.'

The Nanny swayed perceptibly, and Rufus walked
seriously over to where his father was sitting, and gave him
an oddly formal embrace.

'Hello, Rufous Whistler,' said Tristram, calling him by
the pet name they had discovered once in the children's Book
of Birds. 'Everything all right?'

'Everything, thank you,' said the little boy. 'All present
and correct.'

But to Thomas something seemed to be slightly wrong. He
had the oddest feeling there was something missing.

'Where's the other one?' he said, sensing he was doing
something foolish but not knowing how to stop. 'The kid?'

'Other one?' said Rufus.

26

So they hadn't come for him.

After all the horrible waiting, they'd simply failed to turn
up. In the end, he must have fallen asleep. He would never
need the Sleeping Draught again.

He stole a glance across at his brother, standing beside
Nanny (he knew she was leaving because he had seen her
luggage packed ready in the corridor, waiting to be taken
downstairs), but Rufus was giving nothing away.

Adam pinched himself again as he had been pinching

himself since he woke in his room with the screen and the pompom and Beales the Bear, two hours earlier. He had read in some story that pinching was the standard test. Yes, it hurt. He was really there. In spite of that vague feeling of woody swedes in his stomach, he knew it was the Frights themselves who had been taken away in the night. The Frights did not exist.

Strange, though, now he had actually come through it, to find that he felt just the way he did when he gained some unexpected victory over his brother at French cricket, no great satisfaction, almost a sense of apology. Stranger still to have the feeling that, in a mysterious way, part of his life had gone forever − a part that, in view of the terrors which went with it, he was happy to do without − but a loss nonetheless, something magical and irreplaceable now to be exchanged for conkers and cricket bats and all the strings and ink eradicators of school.

As the grownups talked on over the breakfast table, he sneaked another look at Rufus, wondering what new ways he would find of getting at him. There was no doubt that there would be others, but Adam had the feeling they wouldn't be anything like as bad. He might tease or make fun of him in front of other people or give him the Chinese Burn, but there was nothing spooky about a twisted forearm. No, he thought, half of the Frights was in *me*. I was making it horrible. He won't be able to do that again.

The thought made him feel better, and his spirits rose further as he remembered that Rufus was going to boarding school next month, and he'd have the nursery to himself. He could use the best chair, and play with the boats whenever he wanted without bombing them all the time.

Perhaps his friend the American Lieutenant would like to come and sail with him when Rufus was gone. He smiled across at him, the rarest possible gesture of public confidence on his part, and walked up, arm outstretched. No doubt the Lieutenant would give him his customary polite handshake.

'Good morning, good morning,' Adam said, jollily.

The American said nothing, and stared beyond him with an expression of the utmost misery on his face.

Adam tried again.

'Give us some gum, chum,' he said using the fashionable greeting of the village children which no American had ever been known to decline.

Still no response. Adam faltered and gazed around, his confidence draining like Rodgers's sump when he hit the rockery. The grownups were looking at him with the most peculiar expression on their faces. What had he done wrong?

'We don't like little beggars in the dining-room, do we?' said Granny, not waiting for corroboration. 'After all, this isn't the banks of the River Ganges. Or, if it is, someone has been most lax in not informing me.'

Her little jest fell flat, but then it wasn't intended to be buoyant.

Adam thought, the Lieutenant's thinking about something he doesn't like but he can't talk about it, just like I used to be about the Frights. Perhaps I should tell him they don't exist. Perhaps I should tell him they're from inside.

27

They all looked at Thomas as though he were slightly backward.

'I have only one grandson, Mr Lippincott,' said Old Mrs Sanderson, a toothsome triangle of toast and cream and Cutcombe marmalade poised between plate and mouth.

'One's quite enough, thank you,' said Julia with a shudder.

The Italian could not resist a jest.

'I think the gallant Lieutenant, he like to present you with another.'

There was general laughter at this sally, though the Granny did not think it should go too far.

Tristram smiled wanly.

'Are you . . . quite sure?' said Thomas, feeling foolish; after all, they shold know.

'Really, Mr Lippincott, what on earth gave you that idea?'

'I really don't know,' he said.

And he looked around the room in discomfiture, suddenly overcome by a sense of insupportable loneliness and loss, his eye finally coming to rest on Franco's stylish portrait over the chimney piece.

'Only one grandson, you see, Mr Lippincott,' said the Granny, noting his glance, and disposing of the subject as if it were a grape-pip.

And indeed there was only one grandson, Rufus, staring out from the frame with that odd indrawn assertiveness of his, a solitary figure in grey flannels against a background of remembered hills.

28

'Cut along to the Nursery now, and leave Mr Lippincott alone. He has better things to think about than little beggar boys. Come, Mr Lippincott, don't stand there like a duffer. Anyone would think ye'd seen a ghostie.'

Mr Lippincott suddenly fell down, pulling a fairish part of the tablecloth with him. There was a general mélange as Granny tried to save the cream, and Tristram, quicker than the Brigade Doctor, leapt to his feet and rushed to the American's side.

'It looks like some sort of fit,' he said.

'Epileptic, I daresay, grab his tongue with a napkin,' said Granny. 'One really should be more careful who one invites into the house with children around. Still here, bairns? Off wi' ye this instant.'

'He looked frightened to death,' said her daughter-in-law. 'Did he see something? He really didn't seem there half the time. He was always, you know, not quite with one.'

'Taking these, is he, by Jove?' said the Brigade Doctor, holding up the pill-box he had found in the Lieutenant's pockets. 'We've stopped prescribing them over here. Yank overkill, I'm afraid. Mild side-effects . . . narcolepsy, hallucination, that sort of thing. Highly-strung chap, was he?'

As they left the room, Adam thought he detected the faintest trace of satisfaction on his brother's face.

'You know what he saw, don't you?' said Rufus, when they reached the safety of the hall.

'The Frights do not exist,' said Adam, adding authoritatively, 'The Monstrous Crow does not exist.'

'Who said he saw the Frights?' retorted his brother. 'It was your ugly mug that did it. You ought to go round with your head in a bag like a steak and kidney pudding.'

'I don't think he could see me at all,' said Adam, seriously. 'It was all inside, you know. He was too sensitive. It doesn't do to be too sensitive.'

And he put his hand in his pockets like Lord St Paget, and crossed one leg in front of the other in the attitude he called 'Many Years Ago' because of the way grownups talked about the past in front of mantelpieces.

And Rufus didn't say shut up or why are you standing like that with your legs crossed looking like a ruin, but nodded gravely in agreement, which Adam took to be a major advance which all the forces of Field Marshal Ball couldn't reverse.

He uncrossed his legs and swaggered a little, but not too much because it didn't do to be bumptious either.

Outside, the Cutcombe sun was just getting into its stride.

Six Acre, already harbouring a shoal of early mushrooms, swam under a glimmering of dew. Trees stirred beside the Cutcombe River with the torpor of Edwardian ladies, showing delicious legs under long skirts to the trout. And doves in high places poured out an endless propaganda of sounding peace.

True, a county or so away, some two thousand Canadians bound for the beaches of Brittany were addressing themselves to the last Sunday morning of their lives, but no rumour of it had penetrated the wood-pigeon's councils.

'My toe bleeds, Betty,' they crooned to each other and anyone else who cared to listen, at least that's what old Mrs Sanderson said they crooned, but maybe they were crooning something else.

The Universe might be infinitely simple or minutely complex. Time might be bleeding like a pigeon's toe or sprouting and dividing like inocybe patouillardii (Chell's favourite fungus) on a rotten tree-stump, but this, propounded the pigeons, was entirely irrelevant.

The important thing was now.

It was ten o'clock, dragonfly hour, 1942.